Books are to be returned on or before
the last date below.

Alice Thompson's first novel, *Justine*, was joint winner (with Graham Swift) of the James Tait Black Memorial Prize for fiction. For her second novel, *Pandora's Box*, she was shortlisted for the Stakis Scottish Writer of the Year. She has been Writer in Residence for the Shetland Isles and for St Andrews University. In 2000 she won a Creative Scotland Award. Her work has been translated into six languages. She lives in Edinburgh.

PHAROS

Alice Thompson

Virago

A *Virago* Book

First published by Virago Press 2002

Copyright © Alice Thompson 2002

The moral right of the author has been asserted

A CIP catalogue record for this book
is available from the British Library

ISBN 1 86049 949 X
ISBN 1 86049 953 8

Typeset in Melior by M Rules
Printed and bound in Great Britain by
Clays Ltd, St Ives plc

Virago Press
An imprint of
Time Warner Books UK
Brettenham House
Lancaster Place
London WC2E 7EN

www.virago.co.uk

To my Mother

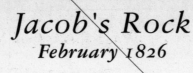

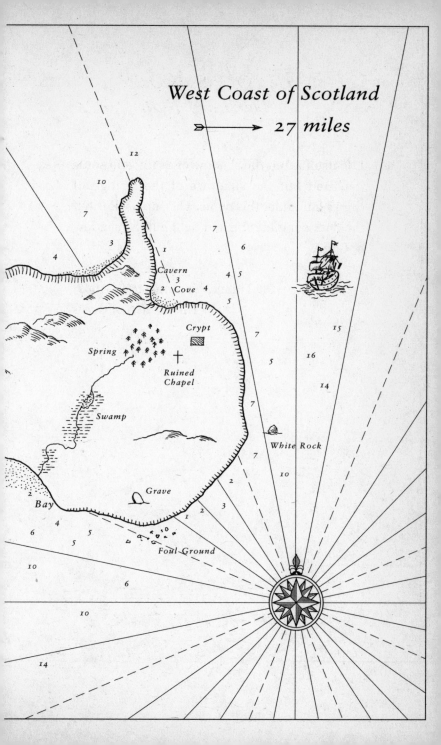

Life itself is but the shadow of death, and souls departed but the shadows of the living: all things fall under this name. The sun itself is but the dark *simulacrum*, and light but the shadow of God.

Sir Thomas Browne (1605–1682)
The Garden of Cyrus

THE LIGHT during darkness must never go out: it was the one cardinal rule of the lighthouse. Whatever happened, the lighthouse's lantern was not allowed to stop shining. It made Cameron preternaturally sensitive to light.

Early in the morning, the sun's rays would reach in through the window of his lighthouse bedroom, while Cameron slept. The beams would stroke his face until sunlight became indistinguishable from his waking consciousness. During the day Cameron would become aware of the shifting graduation from light to shadow and he had to be careful not to let each changing hour affect his mood. He would look out over the sea at noon and see glimmers of light sprinkled across the water's skin and feel a surfeit of pleasure.

1

But at night, while Cameron slept, the candle on his bedside table always burnt brightly. Cameron did not like the dark. Sometimes he felt that he was like the lighthouse: without light there would be no point to him. It seemed to him that if there was only darkness he would disappear into the dark, he would become darkness itself and cease to exist.

Cameron was the Principal Keeper of the lighthouse. He was its life force. God came first, the lighthouse second, and his life consisted of conforming to these two duties. A tall, slim, well-proportioned man, in his early sixties, he walked with his head upright but slightly forward, as if his thoughts came first and then carried him on.

When he looked up to the sky it would be to check the movement of the clouds. He relied on his own eye rather than the mercury barometer that recorded the weather's pressure in a silver liquid line. Clues always lay outside for him: the colour of the sky, the shape and consistency of the clouds, the direction, strength and temperature of the wind.

Cameron had once been a sailor. Often sailors, grown tired of the hardships of the sea, became lighthouse men. Both sailor and keeper were accustomed to isolation and to living with a small number of men. They felt a duty to the paramount safety of the ship and crews' lives. Dependent on the elements, they shared an understanding of the sea, and knew the importance of navigation. Navigation was not an exact science. Allowance had to be made for currents and drifting leewards.

Sometimes Cameron felt that the lighthouse *was* his ship and looking out of the window at the far horizon he could imagine he was on the prow of his boat.

Cameron had a face like a hawk: prominent, fine features which were fiercely symmetrical. The luminosity of his large eyes seemed at odds with the strikingly sharp lines of his cheekbones. His face was mottled brown. His hair was as white as a dove's wing. He had long, thin fingers that tapered to the end as if God had run out of flesh. His light frame belied a strength that was necessary for his work.

He would look into his mirror in his room, the candle flickering beneath it, and see in spite of the shadows around his face a man at the peak of his well-being, and an expression of introspective intensity.

Cameron had respect for the elements, but saw them only in terms of how he could pit his wits against them: he believed that fire, water, earth and air offered up information to him to show in which way they could be defeated.

Cameron seemed to draw his strength from the consciousness with which he apprehended the material world. When he touched the smoothness of the round

3

interior wall of the lighthouse, he felt he was touching the coldness of nature.

The new Assistant Lightkeeper was due to arrive on the rock that early spring day. He was, like Cameron, unmarried. Keepers on island lighthouses were single men. Cameron had thoroughly checked the new keeper's medical records for any history of mental or physical disorder. It was important that the keepers were healthy in mind and body. Their only regular contact with the outside world was the relief boat which came every three months with provisions and letters from the mainland. Even in an emergency the keepers had to wait for the relief boat to send a message for help or to ask for the visiting doctor.

Cameron was looking forward to meeting his apprentice. He had been alone on the lighthouse for a while. The previous assistant keeper had not lasted long. It took discipline to withstand both the isolation and also the close company of others. But Simon seemed, according to his records, strong: he was in his mid-twenties, an ex-farmer rather than a sailor, who would be useful for tilling the small amount of arable land on the island.

The records of Simon's mainland interview, conducted by the Northern Lighthouse Board, had made a particular impression on Cameron. On being asked why he had wanted to work on the lighthouse, Simon had replied, 'Because the work is a matter of life and death.'

Simon would receive the regular annual wage of forty-five guineas and an extra allowance of two guineas for serving on an island. As well as a roof over his head, he would be given fuel, candles, a new uniform every three years and a small pension.

The lighthouse's giant lantern flung its white beam scores of miles over the sea. It was not the strength of the low fixed flame of the oil lamp which give the light its strength, but the lantern's myriad of carefully positioned mirrors and prisms. Sections of the lantern were blanked off to create intervals between the beams. Each lighthouse had its own intervals which denoted the lighthouse's 'character'.

Jacob's Rock stood at a point where three strong currents met over an invisible reef. The island was about one and a half miles long. Jacob's Rock's lighthouse was built on the place of maximum danger, where most people's lives had been lost, most ships wrecked. At the point where boat met stone and the sea swallowed the corpses left behind on the rocks. On a calm day, a smaller group of jagged rocks projected out of the sea, hundreds of feet off the island. More dangerously, on a rough day, these rocks became invisibly submerged.

At the peak of the winter storms, the waves reached up to the lighthouse's top windows, over a hundred feet high, the greater part of the tower disappearing beneath a cascade of salt water. After the storm subsided, the inhabitants

5

of the lighthouse would inspect the ruined island, their vegetable garden wrecked, the grass strewn with shells and gasping fish.

The lighthouse stood on the western point of the island. It looked out over the sea as if it had always been part of the landscape, a natural formation. Its whiteness picked up the whiteness of the seagulls around it, and the white markings they left behind on the rocks. At night the light was another moon or sun in the sky.

Cameron heard voices and looked out to see that the relief ship, broad-decked with a main mast, had moored a few hundred yards off the pier. The voices were coming from a small boat being rowed towards the lighthouse. Cameron took up his binoculars and trained them on the man rowing the boat. It was the relief ship's first mate. He turned the binoculars on the man sitting at the prow. Cameron could see only the back of the man's head, the waves of his black hair just reaching his shoulders. He turned his head as he approached the island and Cameron, training his glasses directly, saw Simon's face for the first time.

There was a strange stillness about Simon's features as if thoughts were the last thing on his mind. He did not look strong, his arms were quite long, his shoulders narrow and his hands on the gunwale fine. Cameron noticed these things without drawing conclusions.

Cameron quickly put on his uniform jacket, and went out on to the pier to greet him. Because of submerged rock, boats could not land on the pier directly but had to anchor ten feet out with man and possessions hoisted on to land by a pulley attached to the pier.

Cameron hauled Simon's belongings on to the island before helping the man himself on to Jacob's Rock. Cameron shouted out a few words to the first mate, who then turned to row back to the relief ship. Cameron picked up Simon's bag. He was surprised by how heavy it was. As the two men made their way up towards the lighthouse, the sun was just beginning to set, turning the lighthouse stone to rose-pink.

They ascended the sharp stone steps carved out of rock to the gun-metal door and Simon entered the lighthouse for the first time. They climbed up the further stone steps that curled round the central hollow of the lighthouse. The pendulum hung down the centre of its space.

The pendulum – a weight on a chain – descended to the bottom of the lighthouse from the lantern room. It was the pendulum that drove the clockwork mechanism which rotated the glass lantern around the oil lamp. The pendulum clicked down an inch at a time as the giant flat cog wheel at the top turned. After a few hours, just as the chain was about to graze the bottom, the cog had to be wound up again at the top.

The pendulum hung in a long vertical line down the centre of the lighthouse like a line drawn in the air. Like an obsession, the movement of the pendulum downwards always had to be at the back of the keepers' minds; the movement of the pendulum in some way always preoccupied them. The click of the weight as it made its way down was a sound of comfort, meant that everything was in order. It was the beat of the lighthouse's heart.

They climbed past the water room, the oil room, the store room and the living quarters, until they reached Simon's bedroom, which was opposite Cameron's. Each of the two higher landings had two bedrooms.

Simon's room was small, with a square window, curved white walls, a table, chair and bed and a worn rug. The sun on the horizon, brimming over the edge, was the only source of light in the darkening room. Cameron instinctively walked towards the window and the light, looked down at the path of light across the sea that led directly to the sun.

At the north-eastern end of the island, at the furthest point from the lighthouse, stood the ruined walls of an eighth-century chapel. Out of sight, between the ruins, lay a rough oblong of stone. The stone was low and flat with black railings around it and surrounded by a narrow ditch. A crypt, about twenty feet long, lay beneath it. Chinks of light fell through the decaying stone roof of the crypt into the interior, casting patterns on the floor.

Pieces of driftwood, the shape and colour of bone, decorated the inside of the crypt. The sides of the inner walls were encrusted with pearly and bruised-patterned shells. Strands of lush green seaweed dangled from the roof, giving the crypt the aura of an underwater cave.

At the far end of the crypt, a young girl was kneeling in the dank shadows. She was wearing nothing but an old ragged white petticoat that emphasized the dark gold of her limbs. Her black curly hair clung tightly to her skull like lichen around a rock. In front of her, on a pedestal, crouched a small ebony statue of a naked man, his mouth gaping open as if the centre of his being was a hole - or he could have been gasping in wonder.

The little girl was in a trance. Her eyes were shut and although her lips were moving they made no sound. Her tongue was flickering in and out of her mouth like a snake. Then, as if she were struggling to speak for the first time, words came out of her mouth, hesitantly and deeply, as if they were made of solid matter.

'It was a small space, not enough to turn in. The wooden ceiling of the hold hovered a few feet over my head as I lay. It was darkness in there. A pitch black, so when I opened my eyes it was as if I were blind. So this was what it was like to be blind. To have one's eyes open and see nothing.

9

'*I could hear the other bodies lying beside me, breathing. I could hear the words spoken in their sleep, the names of daughters, husbands and sons. Names which they would never speak again, except in their sleep.*'

Suddenly the girl's eyes opened wide. They were staring straight ahead. She sat like that for a few moments as expression slowly returned to her eyes and she gradually came back to herself.

During darkness, watches on the light, as if on board a boat, were kept. During the day, the roles of the keepers were clearly delineated. Cameron was responsible for the light, the rota for the watch, the fuel and the trimming of the lamp. Simon's duties included the polishing and cleaning of the windows, especially the dome of the lantern room, and the growing and gathering of food.

At dawn, Simon would walk along the beach on the south side of the island collecting shells. He did not care what kind of shell he found, only that each one was perfect: without chip, scar or dirty mark. He picked up round ones with frilled edges, thin, razor-sharp ones, small snail ones and some so fine that if you put them to the sun they were almost transparent. He picked up scores of shells, dipping them in the sea to wash the sand from them.

Simon also enjoyed catching the fresh food which supplemented their diet of salted meat and biscuits. He fished, put out lobster pots, and collected seagull eggs by getting in a basket attached by a rope to the top of the cliff and lowering himself over the edge. He also tended the vegetable garden on the small, soily patch behind the lighthouse, which produced potatoes and carrots. It was impossible to grow vegetables that reached any taller, or depended on canes, because of the winds.

Simon was fearless. He climbed up cliffs, regardless of their height, and dived off the edge of high rocks to collect winkles from their underbellies. He collected seaweed which would grip his fingers or slide between his hands; sometimes he would, in spite of his sense of balance, trip and fall into a pool of green weed. The slippery texture and strong sea smell reminded him of the act of love. He knew the land and the sea, felt at one with it and forgot himself when he was collecting its food. He saw himself as part of the natural world rather than a man who inhabited it.

The world, for Simon, was not something to be controlled or managed or done to. He had no logical dialogue with it. He moved like an animal, with grace and sinuousness within it. He clambered over rocks with perfect balance, like a dancer, finding poise on a pinnacle of rock, balancing his whole body on an outcrop of stone the size of a fist, or on a cleft edge as narrow as a piece of twined rope.

At night, back in the lighthouse, he lay in bed frightened that an alternate life should have been the one he was living. But when he woke up in the morning and saw the dawn cover the sea he felt content again. There was no doubt life was difficult and solitary here. But on the lighthouse it was also simple.

Cameron enjoyed the night watches. He liked the night stars with the moon high up in the sky, as if he were the only man in this new, strange night world. He liked the feeling of importance the night watch gave him: people's lives depended on his alertness. A ship passed in the distance far away from the hidden reef that spread underwater for a quarter of a mile, invisible just below the surface. The only signal of the reef was at low tide, when the sea brushed its sharp-edged peaks, causing a creamy, foamy ribbon to weave through the curls of the waves.

Cameron looked out at the approximate point where the reef ended and wondered about its treachery. The sea was so calm and immaculate on the surface, the reef lurking like a leviathan beneath it, ready to sink its jaws into the hulls of passing boats. Days later the skeletons of ships would wash up on the shore.

Cameron had grown aware of a central paradox about the lighthouse. The lighthouse was a warning against this natural reef formation and the jagged rocks, but it was also a sign of the reef and the rocks' existence. The light had become synonymous with the danger it represented. The lighthouse kept people away from itself. As it shone across the sea in its generous circular sweep it meant safety and danger at the same time.

And Cameron, alone, watching the still black sea and the full white moon, suddenly wanted the pendulum to reach its end and the light to go out. For things to reach their natural end, and for the reef and sea to claim what was rightfully theirs.

When there was a stillness to the weather, the tower seemed redundant; an aesthetic form, decorative rather than functional. It was as if Cameron and Simon were playing out some elaborate ritual, enacting a religious belief without the presence of God. Only when storms were present did God seem real. And then the function of the lighthouse would return with a force which shot through a keeper's being. But otherwise, there was a sense of waiting and the odd acceptance that when nothing happened, when no boats were wrecked, the absence of events or drama was the point to their existence.

One keeper reflected light, the other the pulse of the body. Like the building, the process of Cameron and Simon getting to know each other was circular. The keepers exchanged no late-night conversations. Diffidence was needed to live successfully together in a lighthouse.

Over the weeks, they rarely argued. They mostly lived in a silent synchronicity. Differences dissolved in the toil of their hands, in the waiting for dusk. In watching the sun set. The rhythm of their life together was hermetic. They lived like monks.

The lighthouse continued its momentum. With a gentle constant throbbing, the pump pumped up oil to the lantern room to feed the lamp and the mechanics of the pendulum ticked the day away.

'There's going to be a storm soon,' Cameron said, looking out to the horizon. Simon looked out but all he could see was a clear evening and the setting sun turning the sea to molten silver. But there were clouds far away and on closer inspection the sea looked slightly more thickly turbulent than he had at first thought. And now a cool breeze was caressing his cheek.

'I might need your help keeping watch tonight, Simon,' Cameron said. 'My vision isn't as good as it was.'

At midnight the storm began to rage. In the lantern room, Simon could feel the waves buffeting the root of the lighthouse, its trunk slightly swaying. As dawn broke, while Cameron was sleeping beside him in the chair, Simon saw in the distance a dark object on the water. A ship was being tossed on the waves, its mast snapped over like a limb broken in half. Having lost wind, the sail was floundering in the huge dark waves crested with dangerous white. The wind was now controlling the hulk of the ship.

Simon put his hand on Cameron's shoulder to wake

him. Cameron slowly opened his eyes and immediately saw what was happening.

Simon could hear the oars creak against the gunwales as he rowed out to sea, as if their small boat were groaning in pain. Cameron, one hand on the tiller, started to bail out the water the sea was splashing in; the sea was beginning to claim the boat as its own. Simon's arms were growing stronger as he fought against the force of the water. The sea was making him strong.

The waves were now veering up on either side of them. Vertiginous sheer faces of rock seemed about to engulf them, then they were going up over the cliff of water, the spray drenching their faces and bodies and clothes. Sea was filling the boat. Simon did not feel the cold. He could only see the light of the lamp hanging from the main mast of the distressed ship between the deep valleys of the waves.

Exhausted, Simon could row no more. Cameron seized the oars and Simon could see the keeper's muscles work with the pulling of the boat as if the oars had become extensions of his arms. It seemed that he was manoeuvring the oars with the power of his thought.

The huge figurehead of the ship loomed up above them. Of a woman's face, her large grey eyes looked out into the distance. The chalky whiteness of her skin shone eerily bright in the light of the moon.

Simon was surprised that he could see no one clinging to the deck of the ship or trying to launch a lifeboat. Cameron flung a rope around the neck of the ship's figurehead, as the waves hurled the two boats towards each other. He attached the rope to their prow. Suddenly, without warning, the ship's towering half-mast came cracking down, splitting its large foredeck in two, the ship folding together and half going under like the studied movement of a dancer taking a bow.

'Untie us!' Cameron shouted, and Simon floundered for the rope which now joined the two boats together like an umbilical cord. He could already begin to feel their prow dipping hard into the sea, trying to follow its mother ship downwards. Fumbling, his cold, frightened hands tried to untie the knot. Cameron shipped the oars and, pushing him violently aside, slashed the rope with a single cut of his knife. The ship disappeared from sight under the water. The keepers scoured the rough seas for survivors, in vain, until the storm drove them back to Jacob's Rock.

The sea, that night, roared and Simon tossed from side to side on his bed as if he were in a boat in a storm. He dreamt vividly and on waking tried to catch his dreams but they slipped through his hands like silvery fish.

The most dangerous place for life on the island was the area of rock that was only visible when the tide was low. This was where the limpets clung. They had to survive living submerged beneath the cold sea and also endure the buffeting of the waves after the tide had receded.

Simon would go down to this no-man's-land to pick barnacles when the tide was low on calm days. He could smell the remains of the sea on the rocks, their dark crevices still filled with sea water, and cold as death. It was a place of death here, just below sea level where creatures hung on for their lives. Their tenacity impressed him. The hardness of their lives had turned their bodies to shells and their feet to rock. They protected themselves against change, against any danger, by turning into stone themselves. Inside their shells, their flesh remained unformed. Their delicate interiors would slip down the keepers' throats like jellied sea.

It was in this inhospitable place, a few days after the storm, that Simon caught sight of the figurehead of the ship lying beneath the seaweed. He pulled, or rather peeled, off the weed, but the plant stuck to the wood as if it were flesh, as if it didn't want to let go. The long green strands gradually revealed more and more wood until Simon realized he was looking not at wood, but at skin; he was looking at the face of a woman. Her dark hair clung to

17

her face closely, indistinguishable from the dark seaweed in the place which was covered by the tide.

He felt her neck for a pulse and his fingertips sensed a faint throbbing. Her neck felt as cold and wet as clay. A closed locket hung from a chain around her neck. He bent down to lift her naked body but she felt heavier than she looked or he had expected, as if she had soaked up the weight of the sea. This caused him to slip as he was lifting her and he cut his hand on the wet, sharp shore, bleeding badly. Carrying her up the steps to the lighthouse her naked legs became covered in his blood. The warm red lines trickling and spotting over her white skin as if drawing a pattern of life over its dead white pallor.

When the woman regained consciousness it quickly became evident that she had lost her memory. The expanse of the sea had wiped it clean. It was not a calm peace that she had been left with. She screamed in the night while the sea drowned her and all her past. She could not say what she was doing in the sea, where she was from or why she had been so far away from land. She screamed for days as if she were trying to give birth to herself. Then she fell silent.

She seemed to have become submerged under an invisible sea. She remained distant from them. She did not speak to them or look them in the eyes. She was like a wild creature they had captured from the water. Her haunted grey eyes looked alert but fugitive. She skulked behind furniture and they could hear her running up the steps at night like an animal uncaged, its energy set loose. Whenever they walked into the room she would scuttle out. Even her ashen skin and facial features seemed evasive, hidden behind her dark cloud of thick, unkempt hair.

She refused to eat with them, instead crouching under their table while they ate. Simon tried to offer her food but she would cover her face with her large paw-like hands. He just left the food on the floor in front of her.

They gave her their cast-off clothes; she buttoned up the loose shirts to the neck and belted the trousers tightly at the waist. She gradually began to respond to requests for help around the lighthouse. She remained silent but would apparently acquiesce to orders.

One morning Simon asked her to bring up some oil from the oil room for the lamps in the kitchen. The oil room was situated in the lower section of the lighthouse, below the store room and above the water room. The pale, white sides of the rooms down below were discoloured and running with damp, the water crystallizing into shining droplets on the face of the wall. The salty, seaweedy odour of the air smelt of the bottom of the sea. The woman held her breath as she filled the oil can from one of the great barrels.

After an hour the woman had still not returned. Simon decided to go down to look for her. He found her standing in the centre of the oil room, her hands over her face, trembling.

'What's wrong?' he asked.

She took her hands away from her face, which had been drained of blood. She looked as if she had seen a ghost.

'There is evil in here,' she whispered. These were the first words he had heard her speak.

She then fainted to the floor. Simon carefully carried her up to bed. She had not developed pneumonia, which Cameron had thought a possibility. Cameron gave her a small amount of laudanum from the medicine chest to dull the trauma suffered by her mind and body.

The keepers considered the lighthouse a safe resting point for her, far from distractions, where she could recover and they could look after her. She was obviously ill in her mind. There was an unspoken agreement between them that she was theirs and it was their duty to protect her until she found herself again. They did not want the outside world to know of her. They felt that secrecy would be part of her recovery.

Over the days she slowly returned to her duties again. But a resilience became apparent which made them wary of showing any gentleness; the look in her eyes could show contempt. She sometimes acted as if she either blamed the keepers for her troubles, or believed that the keepers were hallucinations that her mind had conjured up while she waited for her memory to return.

On the rare occasions when she spoke, it was in well-constructed sentences, which made them think she had been educated in a previous life, a governess perhaps?

The woman looked hard at her reflection in the mirror. She could not connect herself with what she saw; her face could have belonged to a stranger. It was as if she were wearing a mask, for her features could offer her no sense of self.

This made her own sense of self even more amorphous. If she could not believe in her own face, there was nothing physical to hang on to. She was left only with a nebulous spirit. She wanted to reach out to another, but because she did not feel attached to her body, she had no arms or hands for grasping.

As she lay in bed that night, trying to sleep, a knocking kept ringing inside her head. She tried to delete the sound from her mind until she realized with a shock that the noise was not coming from within her. Someone was knocking on her door.

She rose from her bed and went hesitantly to the door and opened it. No one was there. She quickly shut the door. She fell into a fitful sleep where the knockings

turned into the rigging of a ship and the strain of a mast as
they were caught in a storm.

One afternoon, she clambered up the iron steps that led
from the service room to the lantern room directly above.
It was a steep iron ladder and with difficulty she controlled her breathing, for the height was frightening her.
She took a step at a time, forgetting the steps below or
above.

Coming up into the lantern room almost took her
breath away, she was so high up. Looking out around the
sea, the only thing separating her from the drop down to
the rock and the crashing violent sea was a thin pane of
glass. She had to prevent herself from dropping to the
floor and clinging to the hard, real, metal floor. She
remained standing, trying to breathe, looking out.

The lantern revolved slowly on its wheels. The
lantern was huge, built like a hornets' nest of glass
prisms that would magnify the small flame burning on
the paraffin wick in the centre. She felt dizzy and oddly
uneasy, as if she were standing in the centre of space. It
felt unnatural to be so naked in front of the world,
exposed to the sky. Just her, with this huge diamond-like
jewel. And the sea down below, all around, stretching out
to the horizon.

She looked down and saw the waves crash on the
rocks below. The sea was taking her breath away with its

power, as if she were drowning in it, over a hundred feet above.

Lying awake that night, unable to sleep, the woman was sure she heard laughter. A peal of joy that seemed to be giving itself away to the listener. She got out of bed and in her nightshirt wandered out on to the cold stone steps of the lighthouse. She walked up towards the light, the pendulum slowly clicking round, making its journey downwards. She walked up to the lantern room where the mirrors reflected the oil flame rotating, blinding her, and then the laughter again.

But there was no one in the lantern room. It was empty.

Just then she heard footsteps and she flung round to see Cameron standing on the final step, looking at her. In the bright light of the lamp and mirrors his face looked like a death mask.

'What are you doing here?' he asked.

'I heard laughter. A child's laughter.'

His immobile face didn't flinch. He simply looked at her a second longer than was natural.

'It will be the wailing the reef makes. The reef is a hollow cavern. Sometimes the waves, as they rush in, compress the air and force it out, making a howling cry. This unholy wailing warns the ships of the hidden reef. But it cannot be relied upon. Before the lighthouse was built, wreckers from nearby islands would fill in the hollow with boulders to stop its crying. The reef's wailing robbed them of their trade – plundering shipwrecks.'

'But the sound I heard was definitely human.'

'Seagulls can sometimes sound like the cry of humans,' he said.

'But this was laughter.'

She felt angry. His tone was patronizing, implying that she was conceiving fancies in her head. Also, the laughter had unnerved her and she tried to calm herself. But she felt a sudden, irrational, violent urge to push Cameron down the steps. He looked precariously balanced there.

'Laughter can sometimes sound like crying,' he said. 'Go back to bed.'

As she drifted fitfully off to sleep she felt someone climb into bed beside her. She felt someone caress her limbs, touch her hair and face, whisper words in her ear too softly for her to decipher them, but when she reached out, her hands touched thin air. She shuddered. She had felt sure someone had been in her bed, she had felt the touch, but they had been phantom limbs and phantom sweet nothings.

The woman began to wonder what style of clothes she had once worn: a day dress with a simple draped bodice or a dress of watered silk? Had she worn her hair in a plaited knot or in a chignon? Had she been cosseted and vain, or plainly dressed and modest? Her hands gave no clue as to whether her previous occupation had been lady or chamber maid. Her hands had been torn and bruised from the ship-wreck. As soon as they had healed she had tried opening the locket around her neck, the only material clue she had to her identity. But the locket's clasp had stuck.

The woman looked on her own body as if it were some-one else's. She felt she had to reclaim it but didn't know how to begin. In bed, in desperation, she touched her own arms, caressed her thighs, her sex. She ran her hands through her hair, cupped her breasts, but to no avail. She could not seem to make her body hers; it was like touching wood.

She realized that to the others in the lighthouse she was probably even more unreal. How could someone without memory be real at all? She could react to what was around her, but without a memory what kind of person was she?

The next morning she was walking along the beach, looking out to sea, when she saw a small boat rowing towards her. To her astonishment, inside the boat was standing a young mulatto girl, about nine years old, wear-ing a faded petticoat. The woman could not see the lower half of the girl, as the rest of her body was obscured by the side of the boat.

The little girl cried out to her, 'Catch!' and threw the painter towards her. The woman's hands missed it and she bent down to pick it up. When she looked up the boat had gone and she was holding a bit of old rope that looked like it had been washed up on to the beach.

Her mind must be playing tricks on her. Whatever had caused her to lose her memory was now disturbing how she saw the world.

The kitchen fire cast shadows across the round room, the shadows looming out, confusing the imaginary with the real. The woman looked into the blazing fire and saw a face peering through the flames, a face from her past, perhaps, that she could no longer remember. She struggled with her memory but there was nothing she could attach to the face, no context in which she could place it. In desperation, unthinkingly, she put her hands into the flames to try and reach the face, searching for understanding through touch, like a blind person. For a moment she felt skin, then acute pain, as the fire bit into her hand, turning her skin from white to red in a flicker of its flames.

The next day the pain from the burn developed into a fever and she was forced to retire to bed. Late afternoon, someone knocked on the door and she lifted her head from her pillow to see the young assistant keeper enter. Her heart sank. His looks disconcerted her. He had a very still face with green eyes that reminded her of a snake or wild creature, something from the sea. His hands moved delicately, like anemones. As if they had a life of their own, quite apart from the rest of his body, which was lithe and fluid like an acrobat's. His body looked as if it were always alert, as if it were about to jump up and do a somersault in the air, that sitting down never quite satisfied it. But he was sitting down in front of her in the small, round room, on a wooden chair, his hands nervously twisting in his lap.

She wondered what she looked like to him. But she hardly cared and neither, it seemed, did he, as he was acting as if it were quite normal for him to come into a strange, ill woman's bedroom and make conversation.

'Would you like to see a trick? It might help while away the time for you.'

She tried not to smile. Being cooped up in a lighthouse must make people strange, she thought. She nodded.

He bent over towards her and at first she thought he was coming towards her to kiss her, until she saw him keeping on bending, clasping his hands over his head. He moved himself over and round until he was a circle in the middle of the room. He rolled around in the centre of the room like a wheel.

'That's not a trick,' she said rather disappointedly.

Then she watched as suddenly, to her astonishment, he seemed to catch fire. Flames were coming out of his body as he was turning, now on the spot, as if he had been transformed into a Catherine wheel. He lit up the room in the encroaching twilight. Bright red, orange flames spun out of his curved body as he turned and she could no longer see where his head met his hands or even his body at all. He had turned into a wheel of fire.

Gradually his circling slowed down, and as it did so the flames began to die away and she now saw his body, could make out its separate parts, rolling around the floor until his legs uncurved and his back straightened and his head rose up out of the floor and he was standing up again.

The only thing that seemed different about him, apart from his hair having become tousled, was the red glow of his eyes, which she presumed was a reflection of the dying sun outside. The sun was also suffusing the room with a bronze-burnished glow.

Perhaps, she thought, it had all been an illusion and she had mistaken the rays of the sun coming through the window for flames.

'I'm glad I've entertained you,' Simon said. 'I have to go now, as it's supper time. Thank God that the fever has left you.' He made the fever sound as if it was a living entity. He left the room swiftly, and it was a moment before she realized he had gone.

After a week the burn had healed completely but a part of her hand was permanently scarred red, as if it had been splashed by red paint.

One morning the men were astonished to see her come down, having bathed, her hair still damp, and sit with them at table. It was the first time she had joined them to eat. The keepers tried to conceal their pleasure while they and the woman ate together in silence.

Her face had very sharp angles, as if the sea had worn away its edges to the bone. An arched face cut from

28

seashell. A face at odds with circumstance. Her wet hair reminded Simon of when he had found her washed up on the shore. He felt that the past month had been a momentary aberration, and they were back where they had started, where they should have been.

Simon couldn't stop staring at her. Her slate eyes would look at him and then away, unperturbed; as if she were used to such interest. The locket was glinting on her white skin between the open collar of her shirt.

Cameron left the room.

'Have you tried opening the locket? It might be a clue to who you are,' Simon said.

'The clasp has stuck.'

'Try again.'

She put her hand to the locket and it at once flew open. She took it from her neck and peered at the picture inside. It was a miniature of a sailing galleon. The sea beneath it was crested with tiny waves, tipped by white.

'There is something written on its bow,' Simon said.

'Oh yes,' she said. She focused on the minute gold lettering. As she stared, the words became clearer, as if taking shape in front of her eyes. 'They say *Lucia*.'

'Well, we can call you that,' Simon said.

Coming back from the garden, late one afternoon, Lucia saw a man she had not seen before entering the lighthouse. He was a short, burly man with a mass of pale brown curly hair, and a tanned skin which made his pale eyes seem even more piercing. His movements were short and brusque, as if he were moving the air around like bullion, as if the air itself was made of gold. He was wearing a captain's hat.

When she saw him, a powerful sensation overcame her: it was the shock of recognition. She ran into the kitchen to ask Cameron whom the sea captain was that she had just seen enter the lighthouse. Cameron looked at Lucia as if she had lost her mind.

'There's no sea captain here, Lucia. And how could anyone get on to the island without us knowing? You are seeing things, my dear.'

Lucia decided that because she had been tired, the shadow of something substantial on the white wall of the lighthouse had somehow turned into the figure of a man. Or perhaps she had seen one of the keepers who for some reason had walked and looked differently in the strangeness of the light.

The full moon that evening invited Lucia to take a walk along the beach. As she meandered along the shore, she noticed footprints imprinted in the sand. She followed the footprints to the end of the beach where the sand became blank of marks, as if it had been deliberately smoothed over. An object twinkling in the sand, golden in the moonlight, caught her eye. She picked it up: it was a golden guinea. What was a golden guinea doing in the golden sand?

She began scraping away at the smoothed-over sand with her hands. A few moments later her hands struck the lid of a box. The box was too heavy for her to lift up so, with difficulty, she levered the lid off. She expected to find buried treasure. Instead, thousands of brightly coloured yellow and orange glass beads filled up every cranny.

Lucia put her hands inside the mass of small beads. Whatever was hidden underneath the beads she could not feel. She did not want to reach out, right to the bottom, for fear of falling into the huge box. She did not want to be buried alive. She put her hands down the sides of the box, feeling for secret drawers, but the wooden sides seemed smooth.

Exasperated at being unable to find what she was looking for, she withdrew her arms and put the lid back on. The sand was already beginning to trickle back down into the hole. She piled the rest of the sand back in the hole, covering the box, and smoothed the sand over.

The next morning, Lucia went up to the edge of the cliff on the north side of the island and looked out over the sea. It was a late spring day and there was a haze of fine mist blurring the line between sea and sky. Then, through the mist, she saw a small twenty-foot sailing ship moored just off the pier. As the mist lifted the ship became clearer, as if someone was drawing it in with darker ink. Then the mist came down again until it was erased from her sight.

Transfixed, she waited on the edge, sitting on the damp grass, until the mist lifted again. The ship had gone.

She looked up to see Simon approaching her. He sat down next to her on the grass.

'Lucia, you're like the lighthouse. You go dark intermittently. And your whole body is empty except for the steps and the light at the top.' He smiled at her. He then stood up and did an acrobatic leap backwards into the air and stood straight again.

'Must you keep leaping about in the air?' she asked, crossly.

'Let me tell you a story,' Simon replied. 'One day a scorpion came to a flooded river. It was too wide for him to cross so he waited by the bank. A while later a buffalo cautiously approached.

'"Would you mind giving me a lift across the river on your back?" asked the scorpion.

'The buffalo was astonished. "But you would sting me."

'"If I were to sting you while you were giving me a ride, then we would both drown," the scorpion replied.

'The buffalo knelt down and the scorpion crawled on to his back. The buffalo began swimming across the swollen river. But when they were halfway across, the buffalo felt a sharp sting in his back. The scorpion had stung him.

'"Why did you do that?" the buffalo asked the scorpion in disbelief. "Now we are both going to drown."

'"Because it's in my nature," the scorpion replied.'

32

In the afternoon, Lucia decided to take a walk down the cliff path that zig-zagged its way to the stony shoreline below. About halfway down, she turned a corner of the path and almost knocked over the little mulatto girl she had seen over a week ago in the rowing boat. Before Lucia could say anything, the girl had turned on her heels and started to run back down the path. Coming to the bottom, the little girl ran out along the peninsula which protruded from the shore below. Lucia followed her down. Clambering over the peninsula rocks, which cut her ankles remorselessly, Lucia reached the end of the outcrop without catching sight of her; somehow the girl had disappeared.

She turned to go back. To her horror her way back had been cut off from the island by the tide. She was standing on a finger of rocks which was rapidly disappearing under the waves. The sea was rushing around her, crushing against the rocks, and was already too strong and violent and deep for her to make it to the island by swimming.

Lucia perched on the highest peak left and watched as the sea gradually covered more and more rock, the spray biting at her legs, drenching her clothes. Howling around her, the icy wind gave edge to her fear. The water was now lapping around her knees. She tried standing and shouting for help but the island seemed so far away.

A large wave knocked her from where she had been half standing, half clinging to the rock, and she was suddenly floundering in the sea. The cold, the violent force, seized her. As she slipped in and out of consciousness, the freezing water seeped into her body and she became it. She felt an odd kind of relief that she would not have to fight any more. Then a man's arms wrapped around her body like metal bars. Someone was pulling her back through the sea to the shore.

Dragged on to the beach, she found herself lying on the sand encircled by Simon, his arms holding her tightly to share his warmth. As the heat gradually returned to her body she became aware of the litheness of Simon's arms around her, the scent of sea from his skin.

His hair had been slicked back by the water, bringing out the odd symmetry of his face. His slanted eyes, his high cheekbones and almost flat face made him look alien. It startled her; it seemed that she was seeing his face for the first time. He looked like a sea spirit in human form. Even his eyes seemed wholly black, the whites swallowed up by the dark irises. His whole body looked sinuous, as if his arms and legs could grow into his body and become one and slip back into the sea, a seal.

This is another one of his magic tricks, she thought; he is trying to cast spells over my reason. She staggered to her feet. The sand felt warm underneath her feet.

Love did not belong on the island. There was no room for it between the hauntings and the elements, the sea and the sharp precipices, the soft sand and black rock. Even the seagulls had to snatch their love on the wing. It was too violent on the island for the permutations of love, even the love of gratitude.

She did not mention the little girl. She thought the girl must be a recurrent figment of her imagination, an hallucination, and she did not want Simon to think she had lost her mind.

On the horizon, Lucia saw, sailing towards the island, a schooner of about a hundred tons. It was far bigger than the sailing boat she had seen moored in the mist, about two weeks ago. This ship had a large gun behind her foremast which turned on a broad circle of iron.

As it was a calm day with little wind, Lucia waited for what seemed hours, until the ship was within a quarter of a mile of the island. She watched as it anchored within swimming distance of the beach. She wondered if this ship was a clue to her identity, perhaps a sister ship to the one which had brought her here. She knew instinctively that making contact with this ship would be against Cameron's wishes.

Having undressed to her shirt, she waded into the water. The distance to the ship was greater than she had first anticipated: the longer she swam, the more the gap seemed to lengthen between herself and the boat. The currents against which she was swimming were tiring her quickly. The ship was a tall ship, its rigging sails flapping in the gentle breeze. The thick dark hull loomed up out of the water in front of her. She could see no crew. There seemed to be no one on the boat.

Seeing a rope ladder hanging from the stern, she swam round to the ladder's end, which was floating in the water. With difficulty, she climbed up the ladder, the wet cotton of her shirt clinging to her body, weighing her down. She wandered along the length of the ship, tentatively crying out, but there was no reply. She climbed down the wooden steps to the cabin.

A smell of paraffin from the lamp hung in the air. The remains of breakfast for a number of people lay on the table. But there was still no sign of a human being. She climbed back up on deck to look for the hatch into the main hull of the ship. When she found it, she tried to lift the hatch door but could not: it had been locked.

She walked along the deck. The wooden boards were hot and dry beneath her feet. Her hands were bleeding from the splinters of the hatch. The sun was at the highest point of the sky and was beating down on her, filling her with warmth again. But she suddenly felt very vulnerable, half clothed on this empty deck. As her sense of hope that this ship could be her salvation dissolved, so did her fragile presence there.

There was no point in her staying on board a moment

longer. She walked to the edge of the deck and dived back into the sea.

Having stumbled on to the beach, she quickly dressed. It was then that she noticed that a word had been engraved in the sand. The letters were over three feet high. They were long and narrow, as if they had been drawn deeply into the sand by a stick. She had to step back into the sea, soaking her boots and her trousers, to find the perspective to read the letters clearly.

The word was running along the edge of the sea. The sea was just lapping around the bottom edges of the letters, beginning to erase them, tickling into the crevices of sand, bringing down the sand into the deep indentations, and filling them out. Soon the word would be covered by the sea completely.

The word read: BELIEVE.

But who had written the word, and to whom was it addressed? Impatiently, she rubbed out the remains of the letters with her boot rather than wait for the sea to erase them.

For Simon, whatever happened was hardly more or less important than anything else. Time for him was a smooth continuum of white, not so much boring as forever interesting. He did not have a consciousness of self that enabled him to feel proud or pleased that he had saved Lucia from drowning; it was just something that he had done. He felt exactly at the same distance from her as when he had first met her.

But time, for Lucia, since arriving on the island, had changed: it was in black and white. Black was her past and white her present. Black was what she had forgotten and white was the experience of life. And she longed for the shadows of things remembered, of being haunted by memories, by the ghosts of her previous life.

The next day, Lucia encountered Cameron on the stairs. There was something secret behind his eyes; they were always watchful, even when they glittered most with good-will. But then he would smile. His power even at its most extreme had the charm of strength, of self-conviction. He had God on his side and he never let anyone forget it.

It was impossible not to admire him, not to find his ability to judge what was right and what was wrong any-thing but seductive. He was a dictator. And he had all the intense charisma necessary to be a successful one, to sustain his position without question, without insubordination.

'So you've still mislaid your memory?' he said in his careful voice. 'Let's hope we can find it for you. Unless of course you don't want it back.'

He had a slow, cold way of talking that seemed to

snake its way along a sentence. It had its own urbane momentum, a kind of rhythmic lulling, unless it caught someone's inattention up short.

'Why wouldn't I want it back?' Lucia asked, astounded.

'You might have something to hide. Everyone has something to hide. Unless they're very boring indeed. And you don't look boring to me.'

The words sounded full of innuendo but there was no suggestion he was flirting with her. He seemed to be making a statement, not a statement of intent.

She tried to change the subject.

'Do you ever get visitors?' she asked.

He laughed. 'Here? Apart from the relief boat or the doctor? Only the DS: the District Superintendent. He checks up on us once a year, without prior warning. To make sure that the correct procedures for running the lighthouse are being followed. To check that the weather vane is being greased.'

Lucia smiled. But Cameron was being serious.

'Everything here – even what might appear to you the tiniest thing – is a matter of life and death. That is why we keep watch, even when the light isn't on. Fog can appear at any time, during the day as well as the night, falling very quickly, without warning, and we have to be ready to immediately turn on the light. We ring the fog bell too, every ten seconds, but its sound doesn't carry far.'

The bell was fixed at the side of the dome at the top of the lighthouse like a church bell.

Cameron would watch Simon tend his garden, come back dirty and exalted, arms brimming with cauliflowers, turnips and potatoes, and think he looked like he had been dug up from the earth too. That he had burst up from the ground covered in dirt, born of the earth. He was not human at all. He was like a shaman who could travel between the worlds of the living and the dead. Simon would look up and see Cameron staring down at him from the window. Simon would smile up at him, his teeth looking supernaturally white in contrast with his muddy face. A satyr, Cameron thought, a pagan god. He is all surface and instinct.

Cameron was wary of Simon's pagan worship of nature, the pleasures Simon took from it. Cameron saw this worship as primitive and worldly, and it disturbed him. He respected Simon's intuitive knowledge of nature, his ability to live off the land, but disliked a wildness he sensed about Simon which he seemed to have caught from nature like a disease. Cameron saw it as a weakness of will, a lack of moral strength, but he had a fondness for Simon too, so he restrained his judgement of him and treated him like a child who knew no better.

Just at the point when the lighthouse light was switched on, at the point when darkness and light were at equal ratio, Lucia was lying on her bed, and she heard a knocking sound again. This time it seemed to be coming from the service room just above her room. The service room was below the lantern room. Cameron was on watch and Simon had been in his own room, directly below hers. She had heard him singing as she had passed his door on the way up to her room.

She presumed the knocking was the sound of the pendulum as it made its way down the bowel of the lighthouse. Or perhaps something had fallen off the table. But there it went again. A crashing sound, as if a small animal had been let loose.

She climbed up the steps to the service room. Everything was polished and orderly. Nothing was lying on the floor. Everything seemed just as it should be. Except that the log book lying on the table had been opened. A white square of paper was protruding from its pages. She pulled it out. It was a map of the world depicting a trade route from the west coast of Scotland to Jacob's Rock, twenty-seven miles off the coast, down to the west coast of Africa, across to the West Indies and then back to Jacob's Rock. She wondered what this map was doing in the service room. She inserted the map back into the log book and climbed back down the steps to her room.

A few minutes later, the knocking started again. She lay on the bed, puzzled, unsure what to do. Then the sounds seemed to turn into distinct raps, as if someone was knocking on the ceiling of her room. It was very specific and loud, as if demanding her attention.

This time the map had fallen on the floor. Lucia was certain she had placed it carefully back in the log book. Bemused, she bent down to pick it up. There was a loud clatter as a pile of boxes in the corner tumbled over. She realized the air had grown very cold, suddenly. She looked at the barometer: it read zero degrees. She could not breathe for the sensation of an evil presence.

Panicked, she fled the room and ran downstairs to Simon's room and hammered on the door. He opened the door.

'What is it? What's happened?' he said, looking at her stricken face.

'Something strange is happening in the service room. Something is in there moving things. Something violent. But I can't see what it is.'

Simon ran up the steps to the service room. She was always amazed at how swiftly he moved, more like a swallow darting through the air than a man running on ground. She followed him into the room. The room was now still but the boxes were lying cartwheeled over the floor. It no longer felt cold: the barometer's arrow was pointing at sixty-four degrees.

'It was reading zero,' she said.

'It could have been a magnetic storm. It would do that

to the barometer. And this made you think you were cold. The boxes were probably just unevenly piled. Are you sure, as you ran out, you didn't inadvertently knock them down?'

'I suppose I could have. But what about the raps? It sounded like someone was deliberately knocking.'

'In Morse code?' Simon laughed. 'There are always unexplained noises in this lighthouse. Think where it is. It's in the Atlantic. It was probably cracking in the joists. Nothing for you to worry about.'

He was still smiling at her, flushed from his running. With his slightly foreign face and wide mouth, he was convincing her, gradually.

'You don't think I am going mad?' she said, suddenly.

'Of course not. Why should I think that?'

'But you don't know anything about me. *I* don't know anything about me. Why should you take what I see and think on trust?'

He put his arm around her like a brother, loose and gentle like a rope.

She woke at dawn and splashed cold water on her face from the bucket in the corner. The sun was shining through the window and the world seemed to have returned to a comforting normality. How could she have been so fearful of such innocuous happenings? The natural noises of a building in one of the most exposed areas on earth, which she had foolishly mistaken for signals of a malevolent force.

After breakfast, she took a walk along the sandy beach on the south side of the island. It was strange, she thought, that no debris from the ship she had arrived in had been washed up on the shore. There were no traces of the ship at all, over two months since it went down. Lucia tried to remember how she had reached Jacob's Rock. What had she been doing in the vicinity of the lighthouse, miles from anywhere? Why had her boat been shipwrecked in spite of the lighthouse? At night, the light was never supposed to go out. In case of fog, there was always someone on watch, even during the day. Where were they headed? Who else had been on the boat? What had been the nature of her journey? The wash of the waves on the beach seemed to mimic the slow, monotonous wave of questions washing over her mind.

At the end of the beach, standing proud in the grassy dunes, was what seemed to be a standing stone. But as she drew nearer she saw that it was engraved with words. It was a gravestone. She approached and bent down to read the faint writing carved into the grey stone. There was no name or inscription, only *May She Rest in Peace* and the age of death: *18*. The grave was neatly tended, with flowers across it, fresh wild flowers that had been recently picked.

It was a sunny day and the small area of grass around the grave seemed welcoming, waiting for her to enter its stillness. She took off her shoes and, carrying them, felt the soft short mossy turf laced with pink thyme beneath her feet. A seal bobbed its head in the still water of the sea.

Suddenly, out of the sky, a tern swooped low over her head, shrieking on a high-pitched note at odds with its delicate appearance. She bent her face down, but this encouraged it to attack the space around her head with more venom, diving again and again, towards her eyes. She put up her hands to shield them. The tern floated away.

She lay down on the ground and watched the tern disappear high up into the sky. In an idle moment she thought this would be a good place in which to meet death. Death could just come down and swoop her away in this place where idyll became timeless and therefore inhuman. This island was not a place for mortals. She slowly and languorously shut her eyes, feeling the sun beat down on her eyelids, turning her vision to gold. When she awoke, a figure was standing above her.

At first she didn't recognize who it was: the face was in shadows, the sun directly above his head, blinding her vision. Since she had slept, the sun had moved right across the sky.

'You're not supposed to be here,' Cameron said quietly.

His blue eyes looked hard and polished. The shadow across his face made him seem mysterious and unknowable.

He bent down and brushed away the grass that had caught up in her hair.

'It doesn't do any good to sleep so near the dead.'

'Who is buried here?' she asked.

'Ten years ago there was a shipwreck near here. The British galley was carrying slaves illegally from Africa to the Caribbean plantations. The naval patrols had chased them badly off course. The ship hit the reef. All the slaves drowned. They went down with the ship, still manacled to their seats. The body of one female slave was washed up on the beach. She was buried here.'

Lucia was just about to ask how the shipwreck had happened when Cameron offered his hand. She took it and he pulled her to her feet in one easy movement. The sudden pull to her feet, the heat, her thirst, Cameron so near her and playing with her mind, made her feel as if she were about to faint. She wanted to lie back on the ground and wait for him to leave her alone. She wanted him to kiss her.

They walked back to the lighthouse through the waning sun.

That night there was a bad storm, and during the watch which Cameron and Simon kept in turns, they were especially alert. Instead of routine it became a challenge to check the pendulum was wound up as soon as it reached the bottom, that the light continued to turn and that the oil did not run out.

At the beginning of June, the two keepers were sitting at breakfast in the kitchen while Lucia slept above when Cameron announced out of the blue to Simon:

'The last relief boat brought a letter from my youngest sister, Charlotte. She will be arriving soon to help with housekeeping duties here. It will please the Northern Lighthouse Board too – they don't like only two keepers on a lighthouse. In case something goes wrong.'

Simon asked abruptly, 'Goes wrong?'

'As happened on Bell Rock, a few years ago. One of the keepers suddenly died of a heart attack. The surviving keeper was afraid to dispose of his colleague's body in case he was accused of his murder. He had to live for weeks with the corpse lying in the sitting room. In the end, when the smell grew too bad, he propped it up on the balcony outside. The dead man's arms hung over the railings, moving in the wind. When the relief boat came they thought the dead keeper was waving at them.' Cameron gave a dry smile.

'And your sister, Charlotte, is she used to life on lighthouses?'

'Up until now, she's only visited briefly. Charlotte prefers the hurly-burly of Edinburgh.'

'So why do you think she has agreed to come?'

Simon asked questions, Cameron thought, with the directness of a child and as if answers could be infallible.

'I've no idea. I think perhaps to keep an eye on me. Or perhaps an unhappy love affair has forced her to seek sanctuary here. Although that strikes me as highly unlikely. She is not the type to let her actions be influenced by her heart. Still, it is very good timing. Either that, or a fortunate coincidence. She can help us look after our unexpected visitor. The situation is highly unsatisfactory as it stands. A strange woman without a memory being cooped up with men she does not know. It is not proper. Charlotte will make a very good nurse and perhaps help our invalid along the way to recovery more swiftly.'

Charlotte arrived on the next relief boat, bringing with her to the island what appeared to be an air of normality. She was a tall, slender and voluptuous woman and although not immediately beautiful – Charlotte's face looked slightly smeared, as if God had finished his creation and then decided to smudge it slightly with his fingertips – she became more and more striking the more one looked at her. As if various faces fell off her one by one to reveal the truly beautiful one, like a snake shedding its skin.

She had dark red hair that fell in curls about her shoulders and a pale face as white as the lighthouse. But sometimes a colouring would sweep over the delicately distorted features of her face like an intense shadow whose cream and gold and rose-pink combined to intensify, to give shape to an expression of watchfulness. Only her wide lips were obviously delineated, from the first.

Charlotte's room lay opposite Lucia's, and the day after her arrival she invited Lucia into her room.

'You look like you have escaped from a lunatic asylum,' she said to Lucia, smiling. 'In those men's clothes and with your hair flowing wild.'

Pulling off the trousers, the white shirt and the men's boots she had had to wear with thick socks to make them fit, Lucia tried on one of Charlotte's old dresses. The dress was of plain wool in cream and grey. It was inconspicuous, functional and warm. It belted at the waist and had smooth dropped shoulders. The dress smelt of tar soap and the faint scent of Charlotte's perspiration. It was only after a day or so that the smell became Lucia's and she finally felt the dress belonged to her.

Charlotte's flat, square-toed shoes fitted Lucia's feet perfectly. Lucia was also pleased with her hair, which Charlotte had centrally parted and smoothed into a plaited knot on the crown.

Charlotte was quick to learn the rules and ways of the lighthouse. She performed the menial tasks on the island with willingness and skill. Whatever she did, she did pragmatically and well and seemed content in her work, which consisted mainly of cooking and washing.

Charlotte moved as if she always had an end in sight,

full of direction for the tasks she was about to perform. There was no affectation to her gestures. No sense of waiting for anything, ever. Time for Charlotte was not stretched out in front of her, languorously or menacingly, nor was it lying in wait ready to pounce. Rather time was something she could call upon at her will, something she could divide up into hours, like pieces of sweet cake.

They would go down to the store room together where Charlotte would pull back the tarpaulin to reveal the stocks of salted meat, flour and dried fish. The food was neatly stacked all round the room on shelves.

She also accompanied Lucia down to the oil room. The presence of Charlotte seemed to cleanse the room of its evil atmosphere.

It was while Lucia was collecting oil from the furthest barrel that she noticed a door for the first time, almost invisible, cut into the side of the wall. She tried its handle. But before she could turn it, Charlotte cried out:

'Don't open it!'

'Why not?'

'Cameron forbids it. It's one of the rules.'

'Rules?'

'Rules of the lighthouse. We all need rules here. Otherwise everything would fall apart.'

Charlotte seemed oddly asexual, as if she were unaware of her body's curves and sensual weight. She used her body rather as a machine: to carry weight, cook food, to open up the heavy black iron door of the stove. She used her body to take her about her daily duties. Her body acted as if it had more important things to do than wonder about sex. The perpetual smell of flour and milk began to hang over Charlotte, and sometimes beeswax when she had been polishing.

But Lucia, when she looked at her, couldn't help but think of sex, with her blood-red hair and her round arms white, as if having been dipped in milk. And she wondered if Simon thought so too. But both keepers treated Charlotte like a pragmatic Madonna: with respect and dependence. All three quickly began to rely upon her as the centrifugal force of the lighthouse. As if her presence had pointed out a vacuum in the lighthouse before her arrival which they had not noticed and she was now promptly filling up again.

Lucia, in Charlotte's presence, began to feel even more ephemeral and marginal. As if she might just float away. She felt that she would have to hang on to Charlotte or she would escape up into the sky. Charlotte's pragmatism reinforced the sense of her own dubiousness.

Lucia began to want some of Charlotte's pragmatism for herself. Lucia wanted to feel weighed down. She joined Charlotte in her preparation of the meals. She began making bread, enjoying the sensation of soft warm dough between her fingers, the fairy dust of flour on her palms. Lucia became very aware of touch as if for the first time.

Charlotte seemed to Lucia to grow into a kind of beautiful fairy godmother, strong yet ineffable. She appeared to be always standing just behind her body. She seemed to offer Lucia her friendship as if it were a bouquet of flowers. Something that Lucia could grasp with one hand or pick her favourite flowers from, a rose here, a lily there. There were no thorns on the rose but neither did the flowers themselves have any scent: they were simply images.

On the east side of the island the warm air suddenly shifted to freezing. Lucia shivered and rubbed her arms for heat. It was then that she caught sight, for the first time, of an oblong rock, surrounded by black railings, hidden among the ruins of the chapel. Curious, she approached. It had started to drizzle and the grass around the stone was growing sticky with mud. She saw that it was a ruined crypt.

She climbed down the steps. The entrance was open to the elements. The rock interior was bare except for a couple of blankets lying in the corner and a little rag doll, its stuffing leaking from its body, sitting on a ledge.

The deadly, still air deep inside the tomb seemed to be suffocating her. And she was sure she could hear the sound of whispering coming from just above the crypt. At first she thought it was the sound of rain or the wind in the grass but although it was impossible to make out words she could definitely hear a language of some kind. A woman speaking, it sounded like the voice of Charlotte, and the light phrases and rhythms and intonation of a little girl replying.

She crept out of the crypt. It was now raining heavily and she could hardly see more than a foot in front of her. A fog had fallen and she could hear the fog bell clearly ringing. She walked round the side of the crypt, which was overrun with weeds and rocks. A ditch ran like a moat around the crypt. She walked right around widdershins.

Either they were hiding or she had been imagining voices. She returned to the crypt. The whispers had stopped. She waited for the sudden downpour to end and venturing out, made a dash for the lighthouse through the dense miasma of grey. The lighthouse towered out of the fog, a dark, tall shape, its details eroded, its bell ringing, swinging from the side of the dome. She ran straight towards it. As she swung the heavy door open, she heard Charlotte coming up the steps hewn in the rock behind her. Charlotte reached out her arm and touched Lucia's damp, cold shoulder.

'I'd get out of those wet clothes quickly, my dear, or you'll catch your death.' She smiled.

Charlotte was surprisingly strong. Her lack of emotions meant there was no drain on her physical powers. She seemed to have no interest in anyone else, or herself, for that matter. She simply helped the lighthouse to continue.

And there was something about her that, tinged with admiration for her though she was, began to disconcert Lucia. It was as if Charlotte didn't have a memory either. That it was of no use to her, that her mind was not for memories, or hopes or dreams, but merely functionary like the lighthouse. Her mind, like the lighthouse, worked to a pattern, responded, but was not sentient, for she never talked about her past or why she had agreed to come and live on Jacob's Rock.

As they were building the fire together in the kitchen one day, Lucia asked Charlotte, whose face was streaked with coal dust:

'Why have you come to Jacob's Rock, Charlotte? Are you running away from something?'

'Actually, I feel like I am running towards something.'

Her beauty seemed to be shining an odd light around her, as if the beauty was greater, more resonant than her simply physical existence. Lucia thought how wrong it was, that this beauty should go to waste on this lonely rock in the Atlantic. That here it was only seen by her brother, child-like Simon and herself. But then perhaps it wasn't a beauty that should be touched.

'Do you not miss having a family? Having a husband to protect and care for you?'

Charlotte did not look up from laying the fire.

'Cameron and Simon are my family.' Charlotte hesitated,

then went on. 'And you are too, now. You know, your presence has had a strong effect on the lighthouse. It is as if we are a complete family. We will be loath to let you go. Sometimes I don't want your memory to come back at all.'

Above, in the lantern room, Cameron looked out to sea. There was going to be another bad storm soon. He told Simon to dig up as many vegetables from the garden as possible, as soon they were going to be ruined by sea spray. They locked the doors and windows and waited. The afternoon was unnaturally dark and eerily windless. During supper the others were joking and laughing in a way Lucia had never seen before. It was contagious and she was soon joining in their pre-storm hysteria, which gave her a sense of warmth and belonging. They were all battening down the hatches together.

That night the storm began. She could hear its sound first. The pulley line far off by the pier began to clink gently in the calm air, like a faint bell of warning. Then the window in her room started to rattle. The sea began to hurl itself against the rocks, hammering at first softly, then more loudly, pounding at the rock the lighthouse stood on, making the lighthouse itself tremble. The sea seemed angry, as if frustrated that this was its only means of expression.

Lucia went to the window. It was a new moon, the time of the worst storms. The sea was now crashing up against the lower wall of the lighthouse. She could not sleep; the lighthouse was swaying with the force of the wind, like a tree.

She lay half awake, feeling the swaying, falling asleep for a few minutes before being jerked awake by a sudden noise, feeling scared and powerless against such natural strength. The storm raged through the night. She suddenly wanted to be anywhere but here in the middle of this storm. How could they fight against such impenetrable force, such dense unknowingness? How could they fight against the forces of nature?

At dawn there was still no sign of the storm abating; the light was barely perceptible through the dark storm clouds, and its roar seemed even louder around her. She dressed half trembling. She then heard a tremendous roar and the room seemed to turn to green, bathed in an emerald aura. It was as if she were underwater. She looked up at the window to see that a wave had reached up the lighthouse to engulf her window. She screamed until the wave withdrew from the window like a liquid tentacle. Water was now seeping through the frame, sea water.

Then there was a knock at the door and Charlotte entered.

'Are you all right?'

Lucia nodded. Charlotte sat beside her on the bed.

'The sea has the whole of the Atlantic to build up over.

It escalates over an area of a thousand miles until it hits a reef half a mile from the lighthouse. The reef then dramatically narrows and channels the water so that when the water hits the lighthouse it is with a force and momentum unique to this place. But don't worry. These storms, no matter how severe, very rarely do any damage to the new lighthouses. They are built concave, to give in to the wind, to sway slightly. The original lighthouses were far more vulnerable. Made of wood, they were fragile. They would snap in half. They were no match for the sea.'

'What happened to the old lighthouses?'

'The original lighthouse on Eddystone Rock, built over a hundred years ago, had elaborate decoration: wrought-iron balconies and railings, numerous cranes adorning the lighthouse for loading and unloading supplies. The architect Winstanley even attached candlesticks to the exterior of the lantern room.

'His lighthouse was a work of art. But there were those who said it would not last, that the building was top-heavy, the trunk too rigid, the structure unstable. To prove them wrong, he decided to stay in his lighthouse during the winter storms. A few days later, the worst storm in living memory struck the lighthouse. The following day the lighthouse and everyone in it, including Winstanley, had disappeared. There was nothing left but the rock on which the lighthouse had stood.'

Charlotte, seeing that Lucia's face had grown pale, laughed.

'But I'm telling you that this lighthouse is *different*. It has been designed very carefully. The proportions are perfect. The architects have learnt from their mistakes.'

Charlotte went to the window and gazed out at the sea.

'The storm is dying down.'

While reading in the kitchen, Cameron sat stock-still, like a monument made of bronze. He would look down at the religious texts, immersed in the invisible, spiritual world which the words had created. The only thing that would rouse him from his reverie was the ring of the bell, letting him know that Simon had finished his watch. Cameron would read for hours either before the fire or at his desk in his room, until Lucia wondered if his reading had become a meditation of the heart, an embodiment of the spirit rather than the mind.

'You must never interrupt him when he's studying,' Charlotte had warned her. 'He is never quite himself. He needs to come out of his own accord. He needs time to recover himself. To get out of the world he has been in. Otherwise he seems lost and angry if pulled out too quickly.'

One afternoon Cameron became aware of Lucia staring at him and he lifted his head from his book. He said in a dry, conversational way, 'You may find living on a light-house boring. Tedium is one of the occupational hazards.

If I were you, I would take up a hobby. Simon has his magic, Charlotte moulds her candles.'

Lucia looked at his thin face and long straight nose, which were at odds with a sensual mouth which seemed to be of a romantic rather than an ironic disposition.

He gave Lucia a restrained smile which didn't quite leave the seriousness of his eyes behind.

'Walking is my hobby,' Lucia said, 'and just drifting around. Indeed, I am going for a walk now.'

Walking along the cliff edge towards the east side of the island, Lucia, to her surprise, saw two figures coming towards her: it was Simon and the young girl. The girl was walking with simplicity and naturalness of movement, as if she were imitating him.

She was disturbing stones that were breaking off the overhang and falling down to the rocks below with a clatter that was disconcertingly many seconds, too many seconds, late – there appeared to be a dislocation in time as they travelled the space, hundreds of feet long, down.

'You're too near the edge!' Lucia shouted out to her. The girl stopped and looked at her with an equanimity which seemed to Lucia at odds with the incongruity of her presence on the island or with the danger with which she was flirting. Indeed, Lucia thought, the little girl was look-ing at *her* as if she were the intruder on the island, or the one taking irrational risks. The curious absence of light in her eyes drew Lucia into them as irresistibly as matter into a black hole.

Lucia turned to Simon. 'You should keep an eye on her,' she said, but to her surprise he had disappeared.

'Where's Simon?' she asked the girl.

'Simon?'

'The assistant keeper of the lighthouse. He was walking beside you just a moment ago.'

'I don't know what you are talking about.'

Either Simon had played one of his tricks on her or her imagination was misleading her again. This inability to trust herself, she thought, or what she saw with her own eyes, made the world frighteningly indeterminate.

'Look at *me*,' the girl said. And she started to walk even closer to the edge of the precipice.

In her imagination, Lucia saw herself trying to grasp the girl's hand, missing her hand, the little girl falling through the air. The fear and panic was visceral. She felt her throat close up, her hands clench. The girl started to jump up and down on the edge of the cliff, do cartwheels, pretend to trip over.

And then she jumped off the edge. Lucia lunged for her but she was too late. Lucia lost her footing and almost tumbled after her but managed at the last moment to regain her balance. She peered over the edge, expecting to see what she had imagined, the little girl falling through the air like a doll. But she could see her nowhere, not in the air or clinging to the rock, or lying on the narrow shoreline below, laid bare by the withdrawing tide.

A seagull wheeled a few feet below the top above a nest in the cliff face. Lucia stood there for a moment, speechless, and then heard a man's voice shouting out to her. She turned from looking over the cliff edge to see Cameron walking towards her. She was normally slightly frightened of his austere manner, his pale face, and his puritanical self-righteousness, but this time she felt relieved.

She waited for him to come up to her.

'A little girl. She has just fallen off the edge of the cliff. But then she disappeared.' This time she had to tell someone about the girl. She no longer cared if they thought she was mad.

'A little girl?' Cameron asked. 'What little girl?' His face did not register any emotion. He was not giving her any of the shock or concern she had expected from him, or the sense that he would take charge of things.

'The little girl on the cliff,' she said impatiently.

'But there isn't a little girl on the island.'

'I don't care if there is one or not. I just know that I saw her. And she fell off the edge of the cliff. And I didn't manage to save her. We must look for her.'

Cameron was finally now beginning to look concerned. But, Lucia realized, concerned about *her*.

'Lucia, you are under a lot of nervous strain at the moment. You don't think it possible that you imagined her?'

He had put both his cold hands on her shoulders, bending his head down, looking worriedly straight into her eyes. She found she could not meet his pale gaze.

'It's not the first time that I have seen her.' It came out as a whisper. 'I've seen her twice before.'

'There is no one here but us,' Cameron said, 'Charlotte, Simon, myself and you. Think about it. How could anyone else get on to the island without us seeing? The pier is our only connection with the outside world. The pulley is necessary to pull people on to the shore because the rocks prevent a boat coming any nearer. Anyone arriving on the island would have to be pulled ashore by one of us.'

'I must have imagined her,' Lucia conceded. 'You're right. I can't be in my right mind. We know this. The fact that I can't remember who I am suggests it.' She gave a sardonic smile.

'Go to your room and rest, my dear,' Cameron said gently. 'It will make you feel better. Soon you will have forgotten all about it.'

So not only have I forgotten my history, Lucia thought, I am now to forget the present as well.

When Charlotte and Lucia were in the kitchen that evening, preparing supper, Lucia said, as nonchalantly as possible:

'I saw a little girl today on the island.'

Charlotte did not stop kneading the pastry. She reached for the jar of flour and sprinkled some on the board.

So Lucia continued, 'She was a mulatto.'

Charlotte took out a knife and drew an oval in the pastry for the pie's top.

'We haven't wanted to tell you before, Lucia. In case we frightened you. But the lighthouse is supposed to be haunted. No one has seen the ghost clearly, its sex, age or race. But it is said that the ghost is the curse of the slave ship that went down ten years ago off Jacob's Rock, with all the slaves, women, men and children, on board.'

'And you are suggesting that the little girl is this *ghost*?'

Charlotte replied, 'I wouldn't like to say. But I shouldn't mention seeing her to anyone else, if I were you. Otherwise the men will think you mad. A doctor from the mainland might be sent for you. And then who knows what might happen.'

'But I've already mentioned to Cameron that I saw a girl.'

Charlotte looked up sharply.

'What did he say?'

'That it was my imagination.'

'Of course it was your imagination. But I wouldn't confide in Cameron, if I were you, as a rule. He doesn't like to be bothered by wild imaginings.'

'But I did see her, Charlotte.'

'Well, no one else has seen her. If it wasn't a ghost, it

would have been your mind playing tricks on you. Or else Simon is: with his puppets.'

'She wasn't a puppet.'

'They can be very life-like. You probably don't realize how skilled he is.'

'It wasn't a puppet. Nor was it a ghost. I felt her hands. They were of flesh and bone. Besides, puppets can't run without strings.'

'It wouldn't surprise me if Simon could bring inanimate objects to life,' Charlotte said with a large smile. 'Being the animist he is.'

Charlotte looked so real standing there, her hands covered in flour, white dabs on her forehead and cheeks, her red hair tied carelessly back. She looked dense and solid in contrast to these conjectural words. As if Charlotte's persona itself was offering a contradiction to Lucia's imaginings or Charlotte's own talk of ghosts. Charlotte went up to Lucia and hugged her: Charlotte smelt of milk and butter. Lucia wanted to believe Charlotte, wanted to believe in any explanation given her.

And as Charlotte hugged her, Lucia gave in to her, felt her comforting seeping through her, until she herself became its hard fact. Until she heard Charlotte say quietly in her ear:

'You know, Lucia, we are worried about you. Cameron especially. He thinks because of your loss of memory you are very vulnerable. Without a memory you are in the dark. And Cameron believes that the devil lies in the darkness.'

Lucia retired to bed, where she tried in vain to sleep. A sudden noise made her open her eyes in shock. A dark figure was standing at the end of her bed. She was so frightened she could not move.

The cloud left the full moon and she could make out in the moonlight his features, the shadows of the cloud crossing the moon crossing his face. It was Simon.

'What are you doing here?' she hissed.

Her eyes were slitted in anger. The sheet was clenched up to her neck.

'Get out,' she said. 'Get OUT.'

He looked hurt. He put an object down on the end of her bed and walked out. After he had closed the door behind him, she stretched over and picked it up: it was a book. It was a blank book. How dare he give her a blank book? What was he trying to say? She started tearing at it, ripping some of the pages out and then tearing them in halves, quarters and eighths until there was a pile of fine paper like tissue on the bed. She felt as she tore that it was herself she was ripping up, tearing into tiny pieces. She then swept the little piles off the coverlet and they fluttered like leaves of ash on to the floor.

From the small window of his bedroom next morning, Simon looked down outside. He noted the shape of her body, now that she could not see him looking at her. He saw her narrow waist accentuated by wide hips. The sky framed the back of Lucia's dark black hair. Her brooding presence and strong, heavy attire and outline reminded him of a raven. What was she doing here? On a rock island, in the middle of the sea.

Lucia had made her way down to the beach to see if she could find any remains of the wreck of the ship that had brought her here. She found pieces of wood like bone strewn upon the beach. But they had not come from a recent wreck. She was beginning to wonder if she had arrived on a ghost ship.

She picked the old limbs of wood up, cutting her hands on the nails, and carried them up to her room. She placed them around the room like abstract statues. She started to carve a piece of wood, and to her surprise she kept on carving the same object. Her representation was precise and intricate: a small model of a ship, a galley ship. Soon many small ships were dotted about her room. It was her memory trying to get out, she thought, through her hands.

Cameron was on light watch. The hours were rigid, set like the military manoeuvres of a war. Only in the case of life or death would Cameron leave his watch and the room. If he left the room or fell asleep he would automatically lose his job. But that was not why he could be relied upon to be there, and alert. It was because Cameron's sense of duty was as hard as the rock the lighthouse was built upon.

Lucia took this moment to creep into his bedroom. The bed was neatly made. Everything was tidy and contained. A map of the stars was on the wall, the distance between each star and the earth mapped with a line and a number, crossing the map like spokes on a wheel. There was also the daily log book that he kept of the weather, and events that day, lying on the desk. The log that was normally kept in the service room. It was bound in black leather, with the quill not in the inkwell but to the book's side, directly perpendicular. She wondered at the ritual of human beings, to order their worlds, to make sense of chaos, with the position of a pen.

She moved the quill to a diagonal.

It was very silent here. She couldn't hear the turn of the light or the clicking of the pendulum. She imagined Cameron still sitting in the lantern room looking out over the horizon.

She turned to leave the room. She leapt back in shock. Cameron was standing in the doorway.

His face as always was unreadable. She gave a gasp, not so much at the shock of being found as of surprise that he had left his post. He was like a ghost. How could he be in two places at the same time?

'I thought you would be on watch,' she said, trying to accuse him of being in the wrong place at the wrong time to deflect from the fact that she was too.

'Simon has just taken over. You've obviously been in my room longer than you intended.'

He stood there, waiting. Waiting for her to say something, which she knew would just make matters worse. She had broken one of the rules. She had not only invaded his personal life but threatened his ability to do his job well. Absolute trust of the others on the lighthouse was necessary and she would have affected his state of mind. She said nothing.

To her surprise he did not lose his temper, shout at her to get out. He simply said, 'I'm not that interesting, you know. I don't deserve your curiosity.'

She just looked at his steady blue eyes and slightly smiling lips, and never had she been so sure in all her life that she was being lied to.

After she had left, Cameron picked up his diary, which was hidden beneath the log book. He proceeded to write.

Lucia has had the audacity to walk straight into my thoughts. Did she read what was necessary? The music of the sea is relentless. As the woman regains her memory I will recognize who she is. I already think I know who she is. It will be as if her memory is forming her face anew, writing her past on it for me to read in detail.

God is the realm of perpetual light. I must retain my vision of light otherwise I will be doomed to this earthly world of darkness where nature is corrupt and the souls of mankind live in bondage. I must reach the place where external form becomes invisible and the internal is dissolved in union with the King of Light.

One morning Lucia was sitting in her room when there was a knock on her door and Cameron entered.

'Lucia, will you come into the kitchen. There is something we want to discuss with you.'

Lucia looked up, surprised, but meekly followed him into the kitchen, where they were all sitting round the table. They had been waiting for her. Cameron sat at the head, Charlotte gave her a nervous smile and Simon looked ill at ease. Cameron motioned Lucia to sit down next to him. Lucia restrained an urge to run out of the room.

'We are all worried at how you are fitting in here,' Cameron said lugubriously. 'You seem to be wandering about with nothing much to do. You are completely at a loose end. We would like you to fit in more with our way of life. For as long as you are here.'

Lucia nodded.

'So I have drawn up a rota of further duties.'

Lucia picked it up without glancing at it and stood up.

'Oh, and there's something else,' Cameron said. 'We each have our private life here. It is good not to be too intrusive into our own personal matters. We work together on the lighthouse. We have a sense of community. But we also value our privacy. Do you understand?'

She nodded.

She went to her room. She thought bitterly, it is like a prison here. These people if they wish can give me orders. If necessary, perhaps, lock me up. I don't know who they really are. They could be phantoms. The smooth running of the lighthouse seems to be their only motivation. That is the only thing that keeps them together. Otherwise, this lighthouse is empty of love.

I have no privacy to protect. I have no secrets. Or none that I know of. Is that what makes me so curious about other people's secrets? So fearless? Because I have none of my own.

All these psyches in the same lighthouse wanting me for themselves, wanting to mould me, be for them what I cannot be for myself. They bear the mask of strong character: Charlotte's pragmatism, Simon's animism, Cameron's puritanism. What has happened to their private needs and desires?

And I am in the middle trying to recover my own character, which seems tenuous and amorphous; not mine yet. I want to fight off the invasions of these other characters, whose qualities are surreptitiously seeping into my own consciousness. I am powerless over their secret desires.

She picked up the ripped blank book that Simon had given her. There were still pages remaining. She opened it up. She headed the first page, *The Book of False Memories*, and then wrote underneath:

There is no wind. Just moments. I look up at the sun through the gaps between the sails and see dappled light.

There was a knock at her door and Charlotte entered. She was carrying a cup of tea for her, her manner gentle.

'Cameron didn't sound too harsh, did he, at this morning's meeting? Because of his position as Principal Keeper he has to be firm. But it's also his way. He's a man of stern principles. He believes he is right. Always. And he is.'

Charlotte put a motherly arm around her.

'We enjoy having you here, Lucia. We really do. We want to help you all we can. Don't ever think differently. You are welcome into our lives. But Cameron was right to demand a strict hierarchy of privacy. He's the same with all of us, not just you. He treats everyone as subordinate.'

Lucia was surprised to see a certain sophistry in Charlotte when she spoke like this. That her outside maternal manner was really a disguise, that actually Charlotte could be persuasive, could with her words change Lucia's feelings.

Lucia started to follow the rota system. It gave her a sense of security, cleaning one morning, working in the garden the next. She began to find the monotonous routine of the lighthouse reassuring. Instead of feeling like a prison, the lighthouse began to turn into a place of freedom for her. She was like a child in a fabricated family, but with no familial connections, no pressures of being loved or loving.

Lucia began to hope, like Charlotte, that her memory wouldn't return. She began to feel that she preferred her past safely tucked away so that she could pursue this life of living in the moment, in the present, secure and free at the same time. Where even her loneliness, including isolation from herself, was a kind of liberty.

The light of the lighthouse kept on sweeping over the sea at night, as the moon rotated around the earth. She felt on the island almost in the presence of God; that she was at the beginning of the world.

A few days later, Lucia was lying in bed unable to sleep when she heard a distant beating sound start up. The low-pitched, hollow noise was gradually becoming louder and louder until its rhythmic energy seemed to be filling her whole room, pulsating through the walls. She quickly put on her gown and went out on to the stairwell. The throbbing beat was oppressive and relentless, ringing in her ears and shaking the floor beneath her bare feet so that the whole lighthouse seemed to be trembling.

The volume of sound drove her back to her room, where she placed a pillow over her head until the vibrations gradually merged with her dreams.

Lucia looked up at the lighthouse from a slight distance. In the sunlight it seemed innocuous, virtuous, white. It seemed, on the surface, a sanctuary.

Then she saw Simon walking towards her. She felt relief. He seemed to be the one thing in this place it was possible to understand. He had an essential goodness, an innocence which seemed part of the nature around him. He had been uncorrupted by experience or thought. Death was not a word that had occurred to him.

He was holding a lobster pot. A lobster lay on the bottom, waving its arms slightly. As they walked slowly back to the lighthouse together, she said:

'Simon, I heard drums in the night. Do you think I must have imagined them?'

In the direct sunlight she thought his slanted green eyes seemed appraising.

But he only said, 'It's easy to imagine things here.'

He looked out to sea. 'Look how blank it is.'

She looked at it. The blankness met the horizon. Sea and sky were indistinguishable and the point where they merged reminded her suddenly and absolutely of death.

On the other side of the island, between the falling strands of seaweed that decorated the roof, the young girl was kneeling in front of a small wooden fetish at the far end of the crypt. The crypt had been transformed again: seaweed fell in transparent strands from the ceiling, wood and shells festooned the walls and floor. For the second time, the deep, harsh voice began to speak through the little girl's lips.

'The water seeped into the hull gradually, seeping in coolly and inevitably. The reef pierced the hull longwise, gashed it open, and at first it was as if nothing had happened. For a few minutes after the first terrible cracking sound, the ship sailed on towards Jacob's Rock and the silent, sightless lighthouse. The ship sailed on over the shimmering surface of the reef, finding deep water again, as if the surface of the sea had made her whole again.

'But all the time the water was finding its way in, cold, heartless sea water, with its own force and volition, needing its own way in. It trickled around the bodies, lying chained to each other and manacled to the side, locked in the pitch-black holds, stacked like hundreds of books upon a shelf. The cold water began to trace my outline as the murmuring of our resistance grew. But the water was just finding its way in.'

The next day, Lucia was in her room when she heard the sound of a child singing somewhere inside the lighthouse. She ran out on to the landing to see, running down the circular steps of the lighthouse, the girl. She caught sight of the edge of a white petticoat disappearing round the corner. She ran after her, going round and round the steps, spiralling downwards until she felt dizzy with the circular motion, but when she reached the bottom of the lighthouse the girl had gone. She climbed slowly back up the steps and entered the kitchen, where Simon was sitting at the table. For a moment she just stood in the doorway.

'Don't you want to sit down?' he asked.

Lucia stared at him blankly.

'What's wrong? You look as if you have seen a ghost.'

How could Simon read her mind so accurately? she thought. It disturbed her. He didn't seem aware of what he was doing. His comments always came out sounding innocent. Was it just an eerie coincidence?

'No. Of course not. It's nothing.' She didn't want to tell him the truth. She didn't want to make Simon deny the girl's existence to her, as the others already had.

'Your memories are not coming back to haunt you?' Simon asked.

'No,' she replied. 'No memories have come back. *Nihil*. Perhaps I need some kind of help to get my memory back. A spell. A magic potion.'

75

'You shouldn't mock,' Simon said.

A part of her wished she could believe in his magic, hoped that his tricks weren't part of a human sleight of hand. And she knew that her disbelief was also holding her back from desire on this island; this disbelief was something dark but was also keeping her safe, like a shadow from the direct heat of the sun.

'The relief boat is coming tomorrow, so we think it would be better if you kept out of sight of the captain and crew,' Cameron told Lucia at breakfast the next morning.

Lucia was astonished. Having almost physically recovered, she had begun to wait for the next relief boat with anticipation. 'But it's my chance to return to the mainland. I know I haven't regained my memory yet but I'm ready to leave the island. Look at me. With the help of Charlotte, my appearance has been transformed. I could pass for a perfectly normal woman.'

'But you're not a perfectly normal woman, are you, Lucia? We think this is a better place for you to regain your memory. You will be stranded in the mainland. Where would you go? You don't even know where your home is.'

'But there might be someone at the port who has been waiting for me to return, these past months. Who knows who I am.'

'It's highly unlikely. The chances are that your family

or friends have no idea where you are. If they *had* known you were at the port, they would have tracked you down by now. It would have been easy. They could have checked the boats that had left and found out the ones that had been shipwrecked. So we can't have you wandering around the mainland vulnerable and alone. It would be dangerous for you.'

'A letter might come with the boat. Someone who knows the boat was wrecked in this vicinity and has indeed tracked me down.'

'Perhaps. But I think we should keep you hidden until we know for sure.'

'But even if it *is* better that I stay here to recover, I still don't understand why I have to be kept hidden.'

'Because you shouldn't be here. And we will get into trouble for harbouring you. There are strict regulations for the lighthouse, and keeping you here is breaking them. Provisions are measured out for three. I would be sacked if it was found out you were here. And you would be forcibly returned, before you were ready.'

Lucia grew even more puzzled. Surely it was not in Cameron's *nature* to break regulations.

There was something in Cameron's eye she had not seen before. A kind of steely intensity that almost seemed mad in its strength of focus. As if what he was thinking, whatever it was, had become his lifeblood. She felt scared. What she had seen as his strength, his dependability, suddenly seemed to have become a terrible weakness. A strength that was too strong for its own good, like a brittle light-house, built straight up and down, that snapped in the wind, the lighthouse not built to give way to the storms.

It was as if Cameron had read her mind, for he continued, 'It is our duty to save lives on this island: *In Salutem Omnium*. We saved your life. It is our work, our way of life. We normally save lives by prevention. You are one of the few lives we have saved from the sea. You are living proof for our reason for being here. Why the light exists. You being here is constant living validation for our work. Your presence reminds us of the importance of it, every day.'

'But I can't be one of your living validations for the rest of my life. I'm going to have to leave the island sometime. When I recover my memory.'

'Of course. But until then we will look after you.'

That evening, Lucia watched the light of the lighthouse encircle the sea. One moment it lit up an area of sea, the next, as it swung away, it plunged the same area into darkness. The light lit up the sea, creating a blue pathway leading off towards the horizon, then immersed the path in blackness as it left the path behind. As if, where there was no light, the sea wasn't just in shadow but had ceased to exist altogether.

Her thoughts turned towards Simon. She noticed him looking at her when he thought she wasn't looking.

She then, guiltily, promptly, remembered her book of false memories. Everything on Jacob's Rock seemed to be about the lighthouse, its past and its present, and the lighthouse had dominated, obliterated her own history. She needed a history. That night she wrote, '*The wind is blowing through me, I hear the creaking of boards, and the sound of singing in spite of pain.*'

She was astounded by her ability to fabricate so arbitrarily, like a child. But since life seemed once removed, it seemed easier to lie. As if by disguising her profound sense of distance from others, trying to disguise it from *herself*, there was less of a gap between falsehood and truth. One now led to the other, seamlessly, like the breaking of waves.

The following day, Lucia heard footsteps and turned to see Cameron come up towards her where she was standing by the window of the kitchen.

'The melancholy,' Cameron said, 'is why you keep on seeing ghosts. The little girl is simply an impression of melancholy. Once you see her for what she is, she will go away.'

'How do you know that I keep on seeing her?'

'I can see her in your eyes.'

'What if I don't want her to leave me alone?'

'Your melancholy is such a good friend?'

'No. But I will miss her if she goes.'

79

'Melancholy is a dangerous friend. She will make you her slave.'

She was walking past Simon's room, later that evening, when she heard voices coming from within. She could hear the soft tick of the pendulum as it clicked downwards and the sound of the light lens rotating on its wheels above. He was talking to someone. But she had just passed Cameron downstairs. And she had seen Charlotte in the moonlit garden. She became overwhelmingly convinced that the little girl had appeared to Simon and he was talking to her. She wanted to confront him with her. Without knocking she opened Simon's door.

Simon was on the bed. On his knee was a life-size doll carved out of wood. He was talking to it. He looked up and saw her. Whenever Simon was playing with his wooden puppets he never looked nervous. It gave him a seriousness of purpose. He was manipulating the puppet expertly.

Its huge over-sized eyes batted at her, a beautiful alien being. It looked not so much like a doll as a strange creature from another world. Its skin was pale and mobile as if real skin had been stretched over its mechanical skeleton, and the hair had the softness of real dark baby down. She looked more closely at its features. The more she stared at them, the more they seemed to take on a distinct form. With a shock, she finally recognized the shape of her own face looking back at her. The doll had her face.

She did not ask him why. She realized that line of questioning would get her nowhere. It was like everything else in the lighthouse. As if to ask questions, or even worse, to receive answers, would bring the edifice smashing down. She sensed that here, reality was too much to bear, and if conjured up would inevitably destroy everything. Illusion maintained the continuum, the light turning, the men at sea safe. So instead she asked, 'What were you saying to it?'

'I wasn't saying anything to it. It was the doll speaking.'

At least he doesn't think it's human, she thought. But his seriousness, as if it were God-given, made her give a nervous laugh. She felt stupid and tense just standing there.

Simon put the doll down on the floor. It lay there, its dress slightly crumpled. She saw how carefully crafted it was. To her surprise it was double-faced. The back of its head was blank. Her heart stopped for a moment with fear and distaste. At the same moment, before she could stop Simon, he had stood up and kissed her. She felt his lips, his tongue in the distant way of the unaroused: a polite indifference. He knew immediately. He stood back and turned away to let her leave the room.

It was a grey, still morning and the sky had a luminous quality to it, as if the July sun were trying to break through from above. Lucia was walking along the beach when she saw Simon bending down over the sand. He left the spot without seeing her, and she went over to where he had been. She noticed there was an area of disturbed sand: streaks of paler dry sand mixed with the darker, damper, and she dug down with her hands.

Two feet down she struck what she thought was a wooden chest. Brushing the sand away from the object, she uncovered the doll lying at the bottom of the two-foot pit. Its face – her face – looking now straight up at the sky from its sandy grave. Sand was in its eyes and its brightly coloured lips. The legs and arms had been broken so they hung like snapped matchsticks. The dress had been ripped to shreds. She piled the sand back on the doll, filling in the pit. He knew, she thought, knew that she wasn't for real.

Lucia continued on her walk. The sun came out, the bay was still. Looking out to sea from the beach, she saw what she thought, at first, was a seal, bobbing in the water. But it was the head of a woman with long hair who was swimming quite far out. It was Charlotte. Lucia noticed a pile of Charlotte's clothes, neatly folded, on the sand.

On this island, Lucia thought, there were different rules, beneath the rigid rules of the lighthouse. Rules that were the demands of nature and the sea and which superseded the rules of her century's etiquette, or even Charlotte's sense of propriety. Here it seemed natural for a woman to bathe naked in the sea.

'Come and join me.' She heard Charlotte's low voice carry over the still water like a whisper. Charlotte's hair was darkened wet like fur, plastered to her head, her pale features making her look more like a mermaid than a human being, more part of the sea than of human society. Lucia could just make out her pale strong shoulders between the gentle waves.

Lucia undressed quickly on the beach, crouched behind a rock for modesty. Her naked body looked strange in the sunlight and open air, as if it were more different and separate from her than ever. As if the body she had always had was not her own. Her nipples looked pinker, her breasts bigger, her hips wider, her flesh whiter and firmer. As if the light of the day was making her body more physical, less simply an appendage or an after-thought of her mind. Like a physical object that she was haunting. She left her clothes behind the rock and walked out over the beach to the sea.

The cold sea whipped about her ankles. The water reached her calves, lapped around her inner thighs, and she was reminded of the phantom's touch in her bed. The cold seemed to stop her heart and she forgot about Charlotte watching her, far out from shore. Instead she was immediately and only aware of the sea's touch and coldness. She plunged in, giving herself over to the cold-ness, and it seized her in its hands, turned her round with its coldness. She loved this sensation of being all cold. Of being in the state of cold. It no longer mattered that she was without memory; it even began to make sense. If having amnesia allowed her to be in the present this much, to be alive and sensitive to the world.

She breathed in and dived underneath. Here it was still quite shallow; she could see through the water to the sandy bottom, see clearly the odd starfish and shell half buried in the bottom. But as she swam underwater, still holding her breath, she could make out a shadowy shape in the water.

She swam towards it, slowly. It looked like a swaying dark plant. But then, as she approached, she saw it was the naked figure of a man. His eyes wide open, grey, the colour of the sea, as if the sea had dyed them, his dark wavy hair floating out around him. His black body was lithe. His genitals floating in their leaves of pubic hair like black anemones. It was as if he was standing on the sea bed, his arms stretched outwards and upwards, as if in supplication to the surface of the sea. Lucia saw that a chain was attached to one of his ankles, weighing him down to the sea bed.

She came to the surface rapidly and gasping for air. She was now out of her depth, and treading water, a hundred yards out to sea. She looked around for Charlotte, but she had gone. She swam back to the shore and lay down on the hot sand, on the ground, the safe ground, shivering, grateful for the physicality of the warm sand.

Putting on her clothes again and walking round the island, she encountered Charlotte, who was also fully dressed, but with her hair still damp.

'You disappeared,' Lucia said.

'Oh, I swam round the corner of the bay. To the side of the island with the cliff. Then walked up the cliff path.'

Charlotte seemed perfectly normal.

'Are you all right? You look pale,' Charlotte said.

'I'm just cold,' Lucia replied.

'You weren't in long enough. If you're in long enough you get used to the cold,' Charlotte said.

They walked back to the lighthouse hand in hand, Lucia deep in her thoughts. Charlotte walked, as usual, as if she weren't thinking at all. The mortal world refracted off her and she off it.

That night, Lucia became ill again. At the height of her fever, she looked up to see Charlotte's pale face peeping out between her mass of red curls like an angel looking down at her, an angel of death. And Lucia had to muster all her will power to remember that Charlotte was human, that she hadn't come to take Lucia away. The following morning the fever abated and she gradually recovered, watching through the window during the day the blue sky gradually turning to black and the rhythmic interplay of the lighthouse's white beam.

At dusk she fell into a fitful sleep while Charlotte sat in

a corner embroidering, watching over her. Sometime during the night the door opened.

'Is she all right?' It was Cameron's voice.

'She's got through the worst.'

'No sign yet of her recovering her memory?'

'None.'

'Thank God. So we don't have to worry about what to do with her just yet.'

'We might not ever have to worry about what to do with her.'

'You mean she won't get her memory back?'

'It seems unlikely. It's been a long while now.'

'So we could keep her as a lucky mascot.' Cameron's voice was heavy with sarcasm.

'In spite of your fears, she doesn't seem like an agent to me. She has a sweet nature. Have you ever heard her utter an angry word?'

'No. That's what worries me. I don't believe in her. Remember, she is not a whole person – she has lost her memory. We are only seeing a part of who she is. Who knows what she's really like? With her memory she might be a completely different person.'

'But without her memory she's not a threat.'

'Perhaps. We don't know. Whatever, we can't afford to let her go. Her memory might return. She will then remember who she is and why she was sent here, and that will mean trouble for all of us.'

The conversation merged with Lucia's dreams.

After Cameron had gone she woke properly to hear quiet gasps coming from the corner of the room, like the sound of someone crying. She opened her eyes slightly. She could just make out Charlotte's figure bent over. She watched as Charlotte raised her head again. Charlotte was laughing. Her sewing had fallen to the ground and she was sitting in her chair, looking straight ahead and laughing hysterically.

Simon would spend hours in his room practising carving the accoutrements he needed for his magic. Puppets, mechanical birds and boxes of all sizes. As an assistant lighthouse keeper he had much time on his hands and he spent it managing to perfect his skills. For Simon it was an act of devotion to create the objects he then brought to life.

The following day Lucia was still convalescing in bed and Simon came in to keep her company. He sat on the edge of her bed and opened up his hand and a dove flew out of it. It fluttered around the room. He opened his other hand and another dove flew out and perched on the end of her bedstead. He then opened up his first hand again and a third dove flew out. Lucia laughed with unanticipated delight. He continued to do this until at least twenty doves flew around the room. They were perching on the furniture, in the air and on her arm.

'Are they real? Or are they made of wood?' she asked in astonishment.

'It is animism; the ability to bring objects to life. A spirit lives in me. It acts through me. It is what I do. I sometimes wonder if that's what I did with you, by picking you up from the shore.'

'But I'm not an object!'

'When I first saw you lying on the beach, I thought you were the figurehead from the ship that brought you here.'

Lucia looked at him impatiently. 'Please let the birds out.'

He opened the window and they flew out in a line, like tiny sheep, and she watched them trail up into the sky.

'How far will they fly?'

'They will be able to get to the mainland.' He paused and added, 'Not like us.'

'But we can, when the relief boat comes.'

Simon looked at her.

'It may be difficult for you to leave this island.'

Simon was fastening up the window. The room was now cold from the blast of air that had come through the window.

One morning, a few days later, there was the sound of screaming carried by the wind from the other side of the island. The cries were lost in the air. They were coming from the crypt. In front of the wooden fetish, the girl was kneeling, wailing and doubled up in pain. A blossom of blood was unfurling across her back, staining her pale petticoat red. The girl was putting up her hand as if to fend off invisible blows from an invisible whip. The blows seemed to stop. She then collapsed on to the floor and, in a trance, began to speak:

'Condensation dripped slowly down the sides of the curved dark walls, the water glistening in the flickering gleam. The dark interior space seemed to expand and contract within the quivering light; there was no other light but the candle here. Shadow and light fluctuated across the small room.

'You learned to handle the whip with dexterity and precision. You could throw the lash within a hair's-breadth of my back, my eye, my arm, without touching.

'Or you could touch me. You could whip me until my flesh was peeling off me like skin off a strange fruit. And my blood seeped on to the floor like its juice. My back became seared and rigid with scars from the nape of my neck to my lower spine. The natural colour of my skin disappeared and was replaced by a streaked and speckled dusty white, a pale flesh colour, scarcely any of the original dark skin remaining.'

That night Lucia was woken in the middle of the night by a soft whispering in her ear. She lit a candle but in the flickering gloom could make out nothing. Then something moved along the side of the wall in a thick, sinuous gasp like molten lava. She stifled a scream.

The door opened and Simon entered.

'I thought I heard you cry out.'

'Over there, by the wall,' she said, under her breath. Simon looked to where she was pointing.

'I can't see anything.'

Lucia stared hard into the gloom but there was nothing there lying against the wall, no monstrous serpent but her own shadow.

When Lucia entered the kitchen the next morning, Cameron was sitting at the table sipping a mug of tea. He looked up at her when she came in. His eyes made her feel self-conscious; they had knowledge about her that she did not. She felt possessed by him.

'Have any memories returned yet?' he asked.

She felt he was subtly reminding her that she was still suffering from some head injury and therefore was not entirely reliable.

So she lied: 'They have, actually.'

'Which ones?' He was trying to sound more nonchalant than he actually was.

'They seem vague. I am writing them all down.'

'That's a good idea. You don't want to forget them again.'

Later that day, she knocked on the door of Cameron's room, and hearing no reply, entered. There was a smell of burning. The room was as tidy as ever. The Bible was open on his desk. She was surprised to see the margins filled with Cameron's tiny, angular handwriting and certain words underlined. She thought it might have been blasphemous to deface the Bible. She noticed beside the Bible his diary, lying open. The most recent entry read:

The realm of mystery and the unknowable is what I must reach. I will not analyse but through meditation on the King of Light wait for God to reveal himself to me. That is the way to perfect salvation. This revelation will give me absolute truth and I will at last have knowledge of reality. The primacy of my experience of the divine within is paramount.

This is more potent than the external testimony of the Bible. How can a literal language dare to speak of God? The godhead is incomprehensible. It exists in serenity and stillness in eternal space. The release of the soul from enslavement to the material world is the final aim of the Gnostic.

That evening, walking up the stairs of the lighthouse towards her room, Lucia felt a sudden coldness. She could hear a voice, a voice of a little girl calling out her name. Lucia's fear was so intense she could hardly move her limbs, as if a weight was pulling her down into the stone of the stairs. She felt her limbs merging with, becoming one with, the stone of the lighthouse.

At the same time her body slowly dragged her up to where the voice was crying out for her. The voice was slowly taking her upwards. She entered the service room where the steep iron ladder led vertically up to the lantern room. She climbed up, trying not to think about her fear of heights, or what she might find in the lantern room. She reached the top of the ladder and climbed into the highest space of the lighthouse, looking out over the still sea. The room was empty.

Her sense of vertigo almost made her lose her balance but she managed by strength of will to remain standing. She looked around the room again. The light was slowly revolving but no one was there. The sound of the pendulum's chain clicked down.

And then she saw her. She was on the other side of the glass dome on the narrow balcony that edged the lighthouse, about a foot wide, which was reached through an entrance from the service room below. The girl's face was pressed against the glass, her mouth wide open crying Lucia's name, her hands stuck to the glass, clutching vainly at it.

'I'm coming to help you!' Lucia cried. She swiftly climbed back down into the service room and opened the door to the outside of the lighthouse. A light wind was blowing. She climbed up the short ladder to the balcony that surrounded the dome. Her concern for the girl outweighed her own fear of falling to her death. She carefully slid along the narrow balcony to where the girl was.

The girl saw her and smiled with relief. She held out her small hand. Lucia stretched out her own hand to take it. But Lucia's foot slipped. Then there was silence except for the wind in the air as Lucia passed through it, down.

As she fell she noticed, in the moonlight, the detail of the wall of the lighthouse, the slight cracks in the white paint. The rush of wind became rapidly more extreme as her dress wrapped itself tightly around her and the air was pulled out of her lungs. The sensation of falling like a stone was like an extreme emotion that racked her body. Now the shore rock below was coming up towards her like a monster rearing its huge, black, heavy head, but the moment before impact, a huge wave crashed on to the rock, turning it into sea, and she hit water, going down deep into cold, stirring liquid.

She felt something drag her feet downwards. She could feel herself being pulled down under the water. She tried kicking her legs but they were trapped by the grasp on her ankles. She kicked out harder, but although she could move her knees, it made no difference to the downward force exerted on her. She screamed and then went under. The water was cold and dark, but as she opened her eyes she could see clearly around her; there was the sound of water gurgling in her ears, but otherwise there was silence as she was pulled down. The water grew darker and darker and she had the sensation that she was watching herself lose consciousness.

A skua walked along the sand a few inches from her nose in the morning light. She had been washed up on to the beach; she must have lain there all night. Lucia staggered to her feet and walked slowly towards the lighthouse. Spotting her from where she was digging in the garden, Charlotte threw down her spade and quickly ran up to her, her face concerned.

'What on earth has happened to you? Your clothes are drenched.'

Lucia just said, 'I fell in. I was climbing over a rock and slipped. Someone or something tried to pull me under. I almost drowned. A sea monster, perhaps? But I'm fine, really.'

Charlotte put her arm around her and Lucia could feel her warm grace surround and soothe her.

'Darling,' she said, 'there are no monsters here. Who would want to do you harm? We are here to protect you. While you recover. It will be the currents. The rip tides are particularly bad after a storm.'

'But I felt literally grasped. Clamped around my ankles. Like leg irons.'

'Leg irons are for slaves. What would they be doing in the sea? It's your imagination. They were hands. The hands of the sea. The sea has greedy hands.' Charlotte looked at her gently. 'Here, let me take you to my room and we'll warm you with some extra clothes.'

As Charlotte led her to her room, Lucia was thinking that this was not the first time the girl had attempted to lead her to her death. The slip admittedly had been her own fault, but it was the girl who had led her out on to the balcony as she had led her out on to the peninsula, or to the edge of the cliff. But why should this little girl be wanting her to die?

Bodies rotted and faded away, broken like pieces of wood, or grew flatulent like decaying blossoms. Lucia felt safer in the realms of the mind than in the confines of the body. Thoughts relieved her. She would slip into them like a child into a mountain pool, the coldness of her liquid ideas easing the heat of the day. As soon as she became aware of her body she started to sink, to gasp for breath. Her body would be the end of her. A recognition of her body was a recognition of death. And she was not pre-pared for an ending.

The smallest things began to make her jump. She thought the shadow of a bird was someone watching her, a flower that caught the corner of her eye a hand. She kept on turning inanimate things into living beings, into a shoulder, a head, a movement to hide away from or, in defence, to attack. From the real world having seemed unreal, it now became very animate, too real instead of being less than it was. The world was now greater, bigger, more frightening, more powerful and unpredictable. Invasive to her senses when once it had seemed immaterial.

The next day, Simon came walking down the beach towards her. Sometimes, she thought, he should wear a jester's outfit: he was a wise fool. As soon as he saw her he gave her a wide smile of open affection. But then he saw her strained, confused face and immediately looked sad. Simon's simplicity was like a Greek mask, with its dual sides, emotion switching from one side to the other, with no graduations in between.

The realization of his simplicity gave Lucia sudden courage.

'Is your magic, Simon, your ability to bring objects to life, part of the voodoo happenings on this island? Are you responsible for the evil presence here? The drums? The snake I thought I saw in my room?' She resisted mentioning the mulatto girl.

To her surprise, he did not look at her as if she were mad. Instead he replied matter-of-factly, as if he knew exactly what she was talking about:

'My magic is elemental. It requires no ritual, or enslavement to a belief. It has no interest in good or evil. Like nature, it has no motive. My animism only began when I arrived on Jacob's Rock and I expect it will go when I leave.'

It was only when he had turned to walk back to the lighthouse that she realized that he had not answered her question.

Inside the crypt, the little girl was kneeling in front of the wooden fetish. She was almost whispering. In spite of the softness of its pitch, the alien voice had the same deep reserves of anger as before.

'I had been host to the voodoo spirits. My sacred body was taboo. And you raped me and defiled the gods. You acted as if my body were nothing to do with me, but was only yours to justify. And I tried to learn the same.

'But inside I knew. I knew that the pain you were giving me became my pain. When really it belonged to you. And I knew I would take vengeance for this. That I would return the pain to the giver when the time was right, when the giver was most ready to receive it, like a lover waiting for his first kiss.'

The following week, a small sailing ship, bearing the flag of Great Britain, moored off the island and a rowing boat was launched. The man rowing towards Jacob's Rock was wearing a smart blue uniform. The polished buttons, bearing the insignia of the lighthouse, twinkled in the sunshine. It was the District Superintendent making his unannounced inspection.

Lucia rushed out of the room and down the stairs, just at the moment when Cameron was coming out of his room. He blocked the narrow way down.

'Where are you going to in such a hurry, Lucia?' he asked.

'I need to help Charlotte prepare lunch.'

She was trying to edge past Cameron's bulk but was unable to.

'Charlotte will manage on her own. You go back to your room. You look tired.'

He was the king of this kingdom, he ran things, was responsible for the lighthouse, she had to obey. It was one of the rules.

'Cultivate an unclouded mind, Lucia. The testimony of the senses changes and the imagination misleads.'

Cameron looked at her intently. His pale blue eyes looked like pure light. There seemed to be no thought or emotion in them at all. Just will.

She turned to go back upstairs again and walked slowly up the steps to her room. She looked out to see Charlotte at the end of the pier.

Reaching for the pulley, Charlotte winched the Superintendent ashore. Lucia saw him shake her hand. Cameron was now walking over the island to the pier.

She could tell by how Cameron and Charlotte were behaving that they were wanting to impress. Their backs were straight, their arms assertively outstretched, but they were also deferential in the incline of their heads and intimate in how close they stood to him. She saw they were acting in synchronicity and it gave her a shock to see them behaving like that. It seemed to her like an act of complicity. She had not thought of them as being alike, but from a distance, from the window, she could see clearly they were brother and sister. They were consummate professionals. It came naturally to them, as if the thoughts they shared were identical.

She wondered if her fear was coming from an aspect of her paranoia. But she saw the brother and sister walking in step with each other, on either side of the Superintendent, the Superintendent slightly behind their step, looking oddly vulnerable, as if he was the one under examination and the other two waiting in silent judgement, and she felt a heightened sense of danger.

She ran out of her room again and down the steps. She needed to talk to the Superintendent, to explain the situation, to beg him to take her back to the mainland.

She was now running across the island towards him. Cameron and Charlotte both saw her and she was impressed by how quickly they reacted by not reacting. Seeing it was too late to do anything about preventing the Superintendent seeing her, they simply wore expressions of expectation.

It was the Superintendent who looked startled. He was a big man, strong, with thick hands and thighs. Balding, he had a smattering of fine fair hair round the sides like a monk. Lucia took an instant liking to him. Between Charlotte and Cameron he looked like a different species; he did not have their intelligent poise and shrewdness but he seemed to have an earnest humanity that made the pale symmetry of Cameron and Charlotte appear distant and cold. She could see Charlotte and Cameron try to tone themselves down, seem less tall.

Cameron introduced her to the Superintendent as if her presence was entirely natural.

'Lucia is my niece,' he said swiftly, trying to explain her away. They began walking towards the lighthouse. She could tell by the calmness of Cameron's manner that actually, underneath, he was thinking intensely what to do about her.

'I wasn't informed of this.' The Superintendent's voice was quiet with disapproval.

'It was a visit out of the blue. You gave me no warning of your arrival, did you, my dear?' Cameron looked at her briefly and then turned back to the Superintendent. 'My brother's wife had taken ill. She had nowhere to stay. They did not want to leave her alone.' Lucia was simultaneously impressed and taken aback by the smoothness of his lying.

'You know, Mr Black, it is strictly against regulations to have visitors to the lighthouse without notifying the Lighthouse Board.'

'We were just on the point of informing you. The last thing I would want to do is go against regulations. Expediency took matters out of my hands.'

'How long are you planning to have her stay?'

'A week at most. While my sister-in-law recuperates.'

'And are you being treated well, miss?' He turned to her.

She could sense the combined eyes of Cameron and Charlotte upon her.

'Very well, thank you, sir,' she replied. She was too frightened of what they might do to speak her mind.

She watched the three enter the lighthouse for the Superintendent's inspection.

It was when the Superintendent was returning to his boat, alone, having finished the inspection, that Lucia ran after him from where she had been hiding in the garden.

'Please help. I know there is evil in this lighthouse. It is haunted. I am not Cameron's niece. I am being kept captive here. They don't want to let me go.'

'And why not?'

'I don't know.' She wanted to cry with relief that she was at last talking to someone who could help her, who was outwith Jacob's Rock.

'So how did you get here?'

'I can't remember.'

She didn't like the way he was looking at her, softly.

'And what do you want *me* to do?'

'Take me away on your boat. Help me escape from this island.'

He put a kindly arm on her shoulder.

'I'll see what I can do.'

She hid behind a rock and watched as he walked back towards the lighthouse. Cameron and Charlotte were just emerging. The DS walked towards them and she heard him say, 'You were quite right about her,' and then they exchanged words she could not make out.

She watched as Cameron and Charlotte disappeared into the lighthouse again.

The Superintendent walked back towards her and she stood up from behind the rock. This time he took her hand. She held it gratefully, thinking he was going to lead her to his boat, but instead he led her gently back in the direction of the lighthouse.

She pulled back and away from him.

'You've been under a lot of strain, my dear,' he said gently. She started to struggle.

'No!' she shouted. 'You can't take me back there. Please. I'm afraid of what they might do. I'm afraid of what I might do. There is evil here. Diabolical evil.'

'You will be looked after well. It's all the strain of what you've been through. Any fear of the lighthouse is in your imagination. They mean to do you nothing but good. You need to be in an environment of security while you recover.'

'What do you mean, recover?'

'You've lost your memory, haven't you?'

'Yes, but that doesn't make me mad.'

'They've explained everything to me. The hallucinations, the ghost of the little girl that you insist you keep on seeing. The strange noises in the lighthouse. All the result of the head injury you've suffered.'

Her first response was anger, that they were lying like this to make sure she could not leave. To make her stay for a reason she could not fathom. Then she felt panic and confusion, as an even more disconcerting thought occurred to her. Did they really think she was mad? *Was* she mad? Her body was beginning to sweat. Her hands were hot. She felt lightheaded with the rush of heat, as if her body were going to leave her behind.

The whole world around her became very clear. The sea was so blue, it seemed to lose all liquidity, become a colour not a thing. The lighthouse was a white streak in her peripheral vision, like a flash of lightning that had ossified. She was turning into ashes and she slowly disintegrated into the earth again.

She woke up the next morning. They must have put her to bed. Her hair had been combed and tied back and she was wearing a white nightgown.

She got up, washed and dressed. The cool water on her face seemed to remind her that she was alive. She wasn't dead. Her flesh leapt up to its coldness. As if the water was creating her skin, bringing her to life.

She went up to the service room, where Cameron was

sitting, filling in the log. After a few minutes of simply watching, she asked:

'What do you write in there?'

'The weather. The wind . . . When dawn happened.'

She was in awe of time being recorded like that, so factual, so real. The elements of the weather being more real and reliable than her past. And this log would last for a long time. A record of time passing. The turning of the earth. Her memory was inconsequential in the face of these data written out carefully in clear black ink between straight drawn lines. They were nothing to do with her, they were not reducing her to anything. They were versions of something else altogether.

She turned to look at Cameron to find he was looking at her strangely.

'Are you all right?' he asked. 'After you fainted yesterday, Charlotte had to put you to bed.'

For the first time she thought he looked concerned. As if emotion had struck him for the first time.

'Yes. I'm feeling a lot better, thank you, Cameron. I expect the Superintendent has left now?'

'What Superintendent?' He was looking at her even more closely now. The look of concern had subtly changed from a concern for her to a concern about her.

'The Superintendent who came to inspect the lighthouse.'

'There was no Superintendent here, Lucia. You were walking on the beach yesterday in the noon sun and

Simon found you collapsed on the sand. Charlotte has been looking after you since.'

Lucia tried to stay calm. Anger and terror fluctuated over her.

'The Superintendent was inspecting the lighthouse. You and Charlotte greeted him. I talked to him. A big man with brown eyes. In a uniform.'

Cameron walked towards her and put his hand on her shoulder. Why did she always feel small in his company, as if she wasn't quite all there? As if part of her had swiftly and unobtrusively departed.

'Lucia. Please. You're tired. You have probably remembered my talking about the Superintendent and it just came up in your dreams as a scene that seemed like a real event.'

Lucia ran from the room, escaping his cold, comforting hands. She ran round and down the spiral staircase out into the still, misty, raining day.

She found herself running towards the crypt for shelter. Inside, she flung herself on to the cold stone floor, sobbing with confusion and grief for a reality of which she had lost hold. The crypt smelt dark and sweet, of rotting flesh and dampness, as if the air itself was a twisting animal that was curling its damp fur around her neck. Then the voices began in her head, whispering, husky and sweet. Just then she felt small hands caressing her hair. She looked up to see the little girl stroking her.

'Please, don't cry,' she said.

'Get out of my life,' Lucia hissed. 'Leave me alone. You have no place here. You don't belong.'

And then, as the little girl looked at her, stunned and hurt, her legs grazed and her petticoat torn, Lucia said to her:

'Get out of my head.'

The little girl looked at her with terror, as if she were seeing madness in Lucia's eyes.

'But it is you who make no noise when you move,' the girl said quietly. She then turned and ran out of the crypt.

Lucia took a long walk, as if she could take the pain out of her confusion by causing physical hurt to her body. She walked until her body ached, round and round the island until anguish transferred to her blood and bone, until anxiety became transformed into mere physical discomfort. She needed to escape from the insular prison she had constructed for herself.

Over the next few days, as if to compensate for her apparent breakdown, Cameron began to offer Lucia the occasional watch. Her favourite watch was at the cusp of day and dusk, as the light faded and darkness began to fall at the same time. When light and darkness imperceptibly intertwined, impossible to distinguish or separate out.

On one such watch, Simon came up and joined her. After they had sat together in silence for a while, watching the light revolve around the sea, he said quietly, 'Lucia, I am worried about you. Charlotte and Cameron told me what happened about the Superintendent.'

Lucia didn't say anything. She did not know what Simon knew, how much he was involved. He had not seen the Superintendent, as far as she knew, so he might genuinely think she was fantasizing. It was only natural for him to believe what Cameron and Charlotte would have said to him.

'You really don't know, do you? If it happened or not?' He was reading her mind again.

She shook her head.

'We all want to protect you. Why should you disbelieve that? You are very important to us.'

After her watch, she returned to her room and wrote in her book of false memories.

I have travelled thousands of miles. And seen many countries. I am covered in the sweat and blood of strangers.

She put down her pen. When she wrote in her book, she felt possessed, as if in a trance. She suddenly felt a nameless fear, as if someone else was in the room beside her, watching her write, actually causing the words to flow.

She went to the window and threw the book out. She watched it tumble through the air and fall into the sea, where it floated like a dead white bird, an albatross, its wings outstretched on the dark flat sea.

The next morning she looked outside again to see Simon undressing on the rocks in the sharp light. He seemed to take off his clothes in one fluid movement. His naked body was more animalistic than human, and she noticed in the sunlight that his body was covered all over in fine hair, like down. She wondered if that kept him insulated from the cold water, as she had noticed on previous occasions that he had swum for longer than she had thought humanly possible. She watched him dive through the water, arching up and down through the gentle waves like a porpoise, the drops of water flowing over his back like melting glass.

A while later, there was a knock on the door and Simon entered. His hair was still damp. 'This is yours.'

He handed her the book of false memories.

'It was lying on the water. Like an albatross.'

There he was, she thought, catching on to her thoughts as if he were capturing butterflies and returning them to her pinned down by his own lips. And now he was returning to her her memories. Although her words were a tissue of lies. The book was sodden; wet and bedraggled. She opened it. The ink had run like tears down the page but it was miraculously still legible.

'Thank you,' she said. She was worried that he had read the entries, even if they were false.

'Don't worry,' he said, looking at her anxious face. 'I

can't read.' He smiled. 'Your secrets are still safely lying in the book.'

He spoke as if words were things locked up in a box.

'Why don't you come out for a walk?' he added.

They walked until they reached the area of grass where the gravestone stood. It was a bright summer day. They looked down at where the woman had been buried. Another bunch of fresh wild flowers had been placed there.

'Who brings the flowers?' she asked.

Instead of replying, Simon took her in his arms. It was what she had wanted. They lay down on the ground together and he began to run his hands over her body cautiously, like an animal trying to work her out through touch rather than thought. Initially he was clumsy; his careful movements, the lack of rhythm to his touch were almost abrasive. But then she gave in to his way of feeling. She sensed the short, rough-tipped green grass under her, the cliff falling off to its drop behind her, and she looked up into the open white sky and felt as if she were falling up into it, this expanse of white light, a light fall.

The next day, Lucia and Cameron were sitting in the kitchen, waiting for Simon's watch to end. Lucia looked at Cameron and realized that he never spoke about his family or past and never invited questions about them either. She knew nothing about his history, his background or who he was.

'Who are you *like*, Cameron?' she asked.

She realized her curiosity had always been there, since the day he had woken her up in the graveyard. Desire had been transformed into wanting to know.

It had not occurred to her that desire and curiosity were just versions of each other. She had thought her desire for Cameron could be sublimated into curiosity, and she would be free of a certain guilt she associated with herself. However, her desire for Simon was something apart. It was a part of nature. An act which had no meaning. Was not weighed down with implications. An act that had been and gone.

Cameron smiled. 'Likeness is a dubious thing. In the Apocrypha, Jesus said to his disciples, "Compare me to someone and tell me whom I am like." Simon Peter said to him, "You are like a righteous angel." Matthew said to him, "You are like a wise philosopher." But Thomas said to him, "My mouth is wholly incapable of saying whom you are like."'

Charlotte entered the kitchen.

'Come up to my room, Lucia,' she said. 'I want to show you something.'

Charlotte opened the door to her room. Lucia gave a gasp of wonder: instead of Charlotte's usual bedroom, sparse and simple, the room was full of candles. Everywhere around her, on the floor, on the sideboard, candles were flickering.

'It's my hobby,' Charlotte explained. 'I melt down wax and turn it into candles. I carve them.'

And as Lucia looked closely she could see that the candles were all carved with faces of strange monster-like creatures, sphinxes, goblins, centaurs, all very delicate and small.

'We all have pastimes here to while away the time,' Charlotte said.

The candles were stained with various colours that seeped through, colours which had been poured into the boiling wax before it hardened. The paint spiralled through the wax, swirling shapes of rose-pinks, blood-reds, sky-blues and golds skilfully marking out the hair of a satyr or the grinning teeth of a gargoyle. The colours delineated the salient points.

'How can you bear to burn them down?' Lucia asked.

'If you don't burn a candle, what's the point of it? It's the function of a candle to give light. My carvings are just decorations.'

The small window seemed to accentuate the bright luminosity of the candles. Lucia now saw that the room was covered in etchings of all the monsters, with the colours carefully marked out in words next to the parts Charlotte had wanted coloured. The details of the etchings were intricate and the candles replicated the drawings perfectly.

111

'You plan the candles in such detail,' Lucia said.

'I have to,' Charlotte said. 'It's not something that comes easily to me. Working in wax involves so many things: colour, shape and design. It has to be all worked out in advance. Look what happens otherwise.' And she pulled out a drawer.

Inside, in the unstable light around, Lucia could make out misshapen fragments of wax. Monsters with one leg, mermen with no eyes, colours in splotches and stains, all over the wrong places, emphasizing the wrong bits, the back of an elbow, the middle of a tail. Swollen candles with no shape, globules like swollen flesh or shards like broken bones.

'These were all the candles that I didn't plan carefully enough.'

As they walked down the stairs into the kitchen, Charlotte shouted back to her, 'Have any memories returned?'

Lucia decided to recite to Charlotte her latest entry in her book of false memories. 'Only one. *I am in calm water. There is the smell of death and violence beneath me.*'

Charlotte looked at her strangely. 'You should not speak like that. You are frightening me. It sounds like you are making things up.'

Of course I am, Lucia thought, surprised. I have to. For I know that in order to leave this island I will have to invent my memories. I will have to pretend to recover in order to get away.

That evening, before supper, Lucia lay in bed thinking. I can't go on for ever not knowing what is going on. I can't continue in this taut limbo land where nothing is what it seems except for the elements of fire, earth, water and air. It is not enough to be living in this world of confusion and magic and not be myself. There has to be a moment where it reaches breaking point. Where my identity returns and the world collapses into coherence again. I cannot live for much longer in this gossamer world of tenuous relationships between shadowy figures where I am the most ghost-like of them all.

There has to be a splitting in this world's veneer, a crack, a flaw, where meaning seeps in, pushes the glassy surface apart by force of its momentum, rises up from the deep and floods appearance with perspective. I will not become just another puppet on a string dancing in front of such magnificent scenery.

Later, during supper, Lucia looked around the dinner table. Charlotte was spooning out vegetables on to plates. Simon was pouring himself a drink of wine. Cameron was cutting up the salted beef. They were all intent on their tasks, like an ordinary domestic family scene. Her surrogate family; they knew of what her memories consisted.

113

Lucia became overwhelmed by a sensation of panic. Standing up from the table, she rushed out of the lighthouse. There was a slight drizzle in the calm, still early evening and she looked up at the sky and felt the rain gently cleanse her face.

Having recollected herself, she returned to the dining table. She smiled at them and they smiled back and their faces all looked kindly and safe again. They did not ask how she was, as there was no reason why they should think anything was wrong.

Then she began to notice something strange. They were not talking together. They were not communicating with each other, and she thought, that's because they don't want me to see them talking together. It's in secret that they talk to each other. The fact that there were no conspiratorial glances, no secrets whispered, just confirmed to her that something was irretrievably wrong.

The next morning Lucia climbed up to the service room, where Simon was polishing the brass of the steep vertical ladder that led up to the lantern room. Simon was the only person she trusted now, in spite of her feeling the evening before that they were all somehow involved. She needed to trust him. In spite of all his tricks, his almost invisible presence, his mischief-making with reality, he was the only one who seemed solid, who had integrity. That he knew about magic meant he knew about reality too. He knew the difference between truth and lies, between fact and fiction, between past and present.

'Something has made me come here, made me get on a boat and come to the lighthouse.'

She looked at his slightly foreign face. The slanted eyes, the flat nose, the wide mouth, the dark skin. The way his green eyes gave nothing away. She could only read his feelings from his beautiful sensual mouth and the posture of his body. His perfect sense of grace and the smell of him, washed clean by the sea, a salty smell. And she looked at him and wondered what miracle had invented him. What stroke of love and luck had come together to create him.

Simon replied, 'I want to show you something.'

He led her down to the living room and bent down in front of the small cupboard nestling in the curve of the wall.

He brought out a platoon of small, intricately carved wooden soldiers, about two and a half inches tall, and put them on the tattered woollen rug in front of the stove. He began slowly to line them up. Her affection for him quickly turned to anger.

'Aren't you listening to me? I need *answers*,' she said petulantly. 'Why are you playing with *toys*?'

Then she watched the soldiers start to move, *without Simon touching them*.

They ran towards each other and attacked, their rifles outstretched, their red costumes bright. They bayoneted

115

and shot each other, until they were all lying on the floor. Simon then picked them up again, lined them up and the same thing happened all over again.

'Death is built into our bodies. Killing is part of our nature. We give birth. We nurture. We die. Your life, Lucia, your memory of it. It's not particularly important. No more or less than little wooden soldiers who come alive and then die.'

'No,' Lucia said, and then shouted out, 'NO! NO! NO!'

She ran crying from the room and, tears blurring her face, down the steps of the lighthouse, down and down, until she found herself in the oil room. She slowly walked towards the door that Charlotte had forbidden her to open. She put her hand on the handle and turned it.

The door opened easily and silently. Inside was a windowless room. There was a chain attached to the wall and a chain next to the bed. Dust covered all the surfaces. It smelt like a mausoleum.

Iron instruments lay by the basin. Knives and forceps. Soiled napkins were piled up in a bucket. On closer examination of the unmade bed she saw the sheets were rust-stained badly with dried blood.

Closing the door of the dark ominous place, Lucia ran to her room. She had to escape from the island. Tearing a page from her book of false memories, she wrote:

Please contact the DS of the Northern Lighthouse Board. I am stranded on Jacob's Rock. Please come and rescue me. There is darkness here.

She rolled the note into a cylinder and pushed it into the neck of an old cologne bottle she had found washed up on the beach. She threw the bottle with all her strength out of her window and watched it float away on the outgoing tide. There was little hope, she thought, of anyone finding it, of anyone understanding where she was. But at least it gave her some kind of hope.

Lucia woke in the middle of a still night and the full moon hanging in the sky drew her to the window. Four men she had not seen before were standing on the beach. They seemed to be waiting for someone. Then, to her astonishment, she saw Cameron striding towards them, his straight, angular body unmistakable in the moonlight. He seemed to give them orders before leading them down the beach out of sight.

She quickly dressed, and climbed cautiously down the stairs of the lighthouse. She came out into the moonlight and crept down on her hands and knees over the dunes until she reached the tall grass that skirted the beach. She lay on her stomach, watching from about twenty yards away.

The four men were digging into the ground behind the

dunes. Cameron, now joined by the captain, was sitting on a rock watching them. Lucia felt the same recognition of the captain that she had felt before. She felt she knew his innermost thoughts. His body, lithe and slightly hunched, seemed to have grown around his secret motives like a root around a stone, distorted and strong. Greed was his natural drive and he liked the feeling of simplicity and straightforwardness it gave to him.

A box, six foot square, lay on the ground beside them. After half an hour of digging, the four men carefully lowered the box into the hole. As they buried it, one of the crew started up a conversation with Cameron.

'The negroes are causing trouble again.'

'On the ships?'

'No, on the plantations. Using voodoo for their rebellions. A white planter has been murdered.'

At the mention of the word voodoo, Cameron flinched.

The captain interjected. 'Niggers are brutal by nature. They're not even human. They are without souls. You can't expect them to behave like us.'

The crew finished burying the box in silence. After they had carefully smoothed the disturbed sand over, the four men stood up and walked over the dunes out of sight, leaving the captain and Cameron behind.

'You have to do what I want, Cameron, you know that,' the captain said to him quietly.

'It is of no consequence what I do. Or what you do.'

'Ah yes, those gnostic beliefs of yours, Mr Black. If they

help you live with what you let happen ten years ago, good for you. Rather believe the world is arbitrary – the work of the devil – than admit one mistake, heh, Mr Black?'

Lucia saw Cameron hesitate.

The captain laughed. 'Ah, vanity. All is vanity, Mr Black.'

She then watched as the two men slowly followed the crew out of sight.

Lucia walked over to where they had buried the box. Using her hands she dug; after a while she struck the lid. She bent down over the hole and lifted the lid up. Inside the box shone hundreds of golden guineas; the glass beads she had previously unearthed had been miraculously transformed. The coins glittered in the moonlight like grains of sand.

Lucia quickly closed the lid again, filled in the hole and smoothed the surface over.

She saw the ship that had brought the captain and his men to Jacob's Rock, from her window, floating in the sea, like a ghost ship. The ship with the gun had returned. It was anchored a few hundred yards off the pier. She ran out of her room and down the steps of the lighthouse. She walked out on to the beach, undressed and plunged into the cool water. The splashes her limbs made in the water, as she swam towards the ship, seemed unnaturally loud in the calm night. She climbed on to the motionless ship.

The crew were probably still somewhere on the island with Cameron.

Taking an oil lamp from the cabin, she lifted the hatch again. It was pitch black so that the oil lamp only illuminated the entrance not the darkness of the pit beneath.

She went down the steep ladder. The boat down below rocked slightly from side to side. There were benches stretching across the width of the boat as far as she could see in the darkness. Blankets lay in corners. There was the smell of excrement and sweat. Manacles, balls and chains were attached to the wooden sides of the ship. Wooden bowls and spoons lay around, licked clean. She could smell the sweat and sour scent of flesh of men, women and children. This was a transport ship. It transported living flesh. It transported human beings.

She heard the sound of feet on the deck above her. She hid behind one of the benches, quickly blowing out the lamp. The hatch opened and she heard the footsteps of a man climbing down.

A shaft of light circled the room, like the light of the lighthouse revolving in the night sky.

'I can't see anyone.' She recognized the voice of the man who had spoken of the plantation revolts. 'We must have left the hatch open. God, the stench in here is terrible. We'll have to give this ship a good clean. We'll be arriving in port tomorrow. The patrols will be about.'

She heard him climb upstairs, and to her horror the lid fell back down again with a crash.

She then heard the clanging of the anchor as the chain was pulled up from the deck, curling down like a thick metal snake into the hull below where she was hiding. She could hear the sails flapping as they were raised. Then the weight of the ship moved slightly to the side as the light wind finally took hold of the sails.

She clambered over the piles of blankets, which clung to her legs like sodden bodies, and made her way up the ladder. She had to act quickly. The boat would not yet be travelling too quickly because it was a calm night. She listened for a moment just below the hatch and could hear nothing. She hoped they were all in the captain's cabin. She took a breath and with all her strength heaved the hatch upwards with her shoulder. They had not locked it and the gap widened an inch. She slipped her hand between the lid and the deck and levered it up. Lucia slid up through the narrow gap. She was now on deck. She could see a light coming from the cabin and hear laughter. The slavers were drinking and eating. An air of celebration hung in the air.

Back over the sea the island and lighthouse were shrinking but they were still within swimming distance. The light was like a huge god that had to be tended and fed. They were the worshippers, the high priests who worshipped the light. She had to return. She ran up on to the gunwale and, without pausing for thought, dived into the water. The sound of the boat moving through the water easily drowned out the splash and the boat, oblivious, continued on its journey without her.

Cameron's eyes were the grey of the sea, the calm before the storm. He had a stern face, as if wrought out of iron stoicism. He looked as if he had seen it all. He looked as if he were waiting for something.

A few days later, while Charlotte was outside talking to Simon in the garden, Lucia quietly climbed up the steps to Charlotte's room. Having opened the door, she looked around the room, not sure what she was searching for.

The carefully carved candles stood around the room, seeming even more totemic now that they were unlit, as if they were watching her. There were a few books on the table and a pale linen dress draped over the chair. She went over to the desk and opened the drawer which held the misshapen candles.

Underneath the candles was a small indentation in the wood of the drawer which she put her finger into and pulled up. The candles rolled to a corner of the drawer as the drawer's false bottom lifted up. Beneath was a single sheet of paper covered in Charlotte's delicately written script.

I need to write this down. If I am not allowed to speak the words out loud I must put them down on paper.

I will say nothing, I will keep his secret safe. After all, I came to Jacob's Rock to protect him, both from himself and others – not to betray him. Cameron is my brother. He is my flesh and blood. But the knowledge of his guilt possesses and festers inside me. The failure of his duty ten years ago was a human mistake. But the path of immorality it put him on, and which he continues to walk along, is unbearable to my Christian conscience. But for his sake I will remain silent.

It was the beginning of a confession. Before she had time to read further, Lucia heard a noise. She let the paper fall to the floor and turned round to see Charlotte standing there.

'Get out of here,' hissed Charlotte. 'I've tried to warn you off. You have no right to be here. You have ruined our secret with your ghostlike ways, drifting through our lives, leaving a miasma of confusion.'

Lucia turned and ran from the room. She ran along the beach, feeling the sand beneath her feet and the wind against her cheek, the soft rain on her face. She turned to look back at the lighthouse. Cameron was standing on the balcony, looking down at the rocks and sea below. His arms were outstretched. She thought he was going to jump. But he just stood there for a few minutes. His arms then fell to his sides and he turned back and disappeared into the lighthouse.

She knew that she had to speak to him. She started walking slowly back to the lighthouse. She climbed up the steps to the lantern room. Cameron was standing there looking out at the horizon on the far side of the room. Lucia said quietly to his turned back:

'There is the malignant presence of a slave ship haunting this island. Because of your evil involvement in the slave trading. I believe the spirit has taken the form of a little girl. She has brought about chaos here. As revenge.'

'Blasphemy,' Cameron replied. 'I am at one with the King of Light. Who or what would dare to haunt me? You are speaking mere superstition. There are no ghosts here. It is not a little girl ghost who has brought disaster here. It is you. A spy for the British government.'

'I don't understand what you are talking about.'

'No, I don't think you do. With or without your memory I am now inclined to agree with Charlotte. You do not have the personality of a government agent.' He paused. 'I will have to look closer to home.' He still had his back to her.

'But you *are* involved in slaving?'

He turned round and looked at the woman and felt that she represented the end of something. He felt resigned to death. He looked out over the horizon and it beckoned to him. It seemed to lie on the edge of life.

'What do *I* have to do with the common laws of our

land?' Cameron replied. 'The material world is contemptible. *For the wholly spiritual all things are permissible.*'

'And Charlotte? How far is she involved?'

He turned round. He was smiling. The light was revolving between them.

'She always was a pragmatist.'

Lucia ran out of the lighthouse down to the shore. She saw the ship lying on the water, like a malignant presence in the vicinity of the island. It had returned from port and would be setting sail at any moment for its journey south. Anger and a feeling of powerlessness forced her to act. She pulled off her dress and, still dressed in her petticoat, waded out into the water. She dived into the water and swam out to the ship.

Over the water, she could hear the crew laughing and singing down in the hold. They were preparing the chains for the human cargo they were about to collect. She climbed up on to the deck, bolted the hatch, locking them in the hold, and went down into the cabin, where she poured oil over the floor and furniture. She piled up the maps and documents from the cabin on to the deck, together with articles of wood, the bead and cotton barter-ing goods they had dug up from the island and pieces of tarred rope. She threw a burning oil lamp on the pile. She watched as the papers were seized by the flames. She watched as the wooden mast of the ship itself began to burn and the corners of the sails began to flicker orange. Because of the reflection of the burning ship in the sea, the water itself seemed to be on fire. She dived overboard, and it was as if she were diving into the living flames.

She swam back to the shore. She staggered out on to the beach and, exhausted, fell on all fours and crawled up on to dry sand. She came upon the feet and ankles of someone standing on the shore. She looked up. Charlotte was staring down at her. The ship was now ablaze on the water. As if the sea itself was burning.

'What have you done?' Charlotte asked.

'What have *you* done?' Lucia asked accusingly.

'You fool. I'm no trafficker in slaves. It is Cameron, and Cameron alone, who has been letting the slavers use Jacob's Rock as a base. They use the island to hide the glass beads and gold.'

'I still don't fully understand.'

'The slavers buy the slaves from Guinea with beads. They then sell the slaves on to the sugar planters in the West Indies for gold.'

'But why bury the trinkets and gold on Jacob's Rock?'

'Naval patrols will search a schooner for evidence. The slavers use smaller sailing boats to take and collect the cotton or gold from the island to mainland Scotland. Small boats aren't searched.'

'And you have turned a blind eye?'

'Cameron is my brother. But I should warn you, Lucia, he has grown deluded and paranoid. He thinks the government has found evidence of the illegal trading and has sent a spy to the island. He thinks the spy is you.'

Charlotte's normally serene features were creased with anxiety.

'But I've already confronted him. I think he now suspects you.' But Charlotte had started to run towards the lighthouse, and the wind was blowing Lucia's words, unheard, back in her face.

Lucia ran after her, but by the time she had reached the lighthouse Charlotte had disappeared inside.

Charlotte climbed up to the lantern room, where Cameron was keeping watch. The look on her brother's face was one of anger and disdain.

'So, Charlotte. You have betrayed me. My own dear sister.'

Charlotte looked at him, her face pained. 'I am no spy. The only person I have betrayed is myself. By remaining silent. Besides, how can you ever be betrayed? When earthly matters mean so little to you. If slave trading for you is just a way of proving how your spirit can transcend the mundane.'

'You always were a sophist.'

'At least I am not a sophist of the soul. If this is your road to spiritual enlightenment, then God forgive you.'

'How can I expect you to understand? Yours is a popular morality.'

'And *you* deal in the enslavement of souls, just as your own soul has been enslaved by your deluded beliefs. It is you who have betrayed me.'

'You are a spy for the government.'

'I am no spy. There is no spy.'

Charlotte was crying now. She watched through blurred eyes as Cameron came towards her. He is going to kill me, she thought. And on this island, there is nowhere for me to run. But he put his arm around her. Her head leant on his shoulder, her red hair falling over the jacket of his dark blue uniform.

'We will wait for the relief boat. It is due soon. You and your government may arrest me then. I have no concern for my freedom on this earth. I bathe in the light where I am perpetually free.'

The lines in his face, all the signals of age, his veins, his mottled hands, distracted her from reading his character cleanly. She saw a longing in his body, a languorous stretching out, and misread it for a desire for life when really it was a desire for death.

Lucia found Simon on the beach.

'Simon, we have to leave the island.'

He looked up from where he was sitting, cross-legged, on the sand.

'I can't leave here. Not now. I belong here. I have to look after the little girl.'

'So she *is* real.'

He laughed. 'Did you think she was one of my puppets?'

'I thought she was the ghost of the slave ship.'

'No. The ghost on the island is not her.'

'So where does the girl come from?'

'Perhaps she should tell you for herself.'

'Grace,' he shouted into the air, as if summoning her up from the invisible world.

The girl appeared from behind a rock. She was holding a bunch of wild flowers.

She looked at Lucia hard.

'Follow me.'

She led Lucia along the cliff edge to the tombstone, where she carefully put her fresh flowers on the grave. Lucia realized by the sadness on her face who was buried there.

'It's your mother.'

'Ten years ago, my mother was the sole survivor of the shipwrecked *Lucia*. Hundreds of slaves drowned. I was born on Jacob's Rock, a year later.'

'A *year* later? I don't understand.'

'Is it so difficult? Do you think that Cameron is not fully aware of my existence on the island? He just pretends not to know. He pretends that I don't exist. My presence here seems to haunt him.'

129

'Cameron is your *father*?'

'My mother died in childbirth. That, and the fact that she was a priestess, is all I know about her. Cameron hid me in the secret room. Then, while I was still very young, Cameron ejected me from the lighthouse. I learnt to live off nature and on my wits, to hunt and to swim.

'I use the crypt for shelter, sometimes steal food from the store room. Simon also helps me. And Charlotte. But Charlotte doesn't know who my father is. I think she suspects but refuses to admit it to herself. Simon knows. Simon knows everything.'

'But I don't understand why you kept on leading *me* into danger. Playing games like that. I would have helped you too.'

The little girl gave her a level stare.

'Because you don't seem natural.'

'Natural?'

'I feel you mean to do harm in some way.'

'To whom?'

'I don't know. All I know is that you don't belong on the island. There is something malignant about you.'

Simon and Grace seemed to be looking at her in the same way: with a mixture of tenderness and fear.

Having arranged to meet Lucia and Simon the next day, Grace returned to the crypt. It was the only place on the island where she felt safe. She knelt down in front of the fetish and fell into a trance. The slavery of possession overtook her again, the girl's identity fragmented and the deep voice spoke through her young lips.

'The voice is dangerous. The voice has an energy of its own. For my words have power. As priestess of voodoo I have need of expression. The compulsion to tell my story. And I speak out loud now what you have done, keeper of the light. I died giving birth to your child: a child of rape.'

At this point, Grace, still speaking in the slow, monotonous chant which only accentuated the horror she was uttering, had tears rolling down her cheeks. Not her tears, for she understood or heard nothing, but her mother's tears.

'But I live on through this voice. My daughter gives me the power of voice. And speaking is more dangerous than writing.

'And I curse you. I have summoned up the evil spirit of the slave ship from the depths of the sea. Due to the touch of the animist, the spirit now roams this island. The evil spirit is now my slave. The spirit makes the lighthouse dream voodoo dreams. And its evil matches your own.

'Can you hear me, Cameron? Keeper of the light? Can you hear my voice?'

Far away, Cameron looked out to the horizon and thought he heard his name being called. He dismissed it as a figment of his imagination.

That night Lucia grew restless, as the sound of beating drums started up again in the lighthouse. She dressed and opened her door. The sound of drums was coming from somewhere down below in the lighthouse, and she followed their insistent rhythm into the oil room. There was nothing in there but the barrels. The beating drums were coming from behind the door of the secret room.

She opened the door. The secret room had disappeared, to be replaced by a much larger room, a room whose size would have been impossible for the lighthouse to contain. A throng of dark bodies filled it. They were standing in front of a raised platform draped with a red and white cloth. On the platform stood a simple white chair on which sat an eighteen-year-old woman. A priestess, she was dressed in a white robe. Her face was covered in a design of scars. Lucia could make out the shape of a serpent interwoven into the pattern.

A low, sweet chant started up and then after a while abruptly ended, as if the chanters had been struck dumb. The worshippers started to pray in silence. Suddenly, the priestess broke their meditation with shouting, hurling abuse at them in an incomprehensible language.

The priestess's staff, in the shape of the serpent, seemed to Lucia to be coming alive and writhing in her hand. Her violent words unleashed a kind of ecstasy in the crowd and the people began to move sinuously.

She stopped shouting and the chanting began again. Dancing started up with loud singing and the whole crowd swayed from side to side as a hysteria charged the room.

The crowd was losing control of their bodies. The gestures of the twisting snake overcame them as they began writhing on the floor.

Silence fell again as two men dressed in red appeared from behind the curtain. The two men led by the hand a little trembling boy in white robes emphasizing the darkness of his skin. The men led him to the throne, where he prostrated himself before the priestess.

Then from behind the curtain appeared a four-year-old girl, also dressed in white. The two men picked up the children, who were struggling, and bound their hands and feet. To stop the boy's cries, one of the men put a hand over his mouth. The little girl was silent.

Each man held up a child by their feet, as if they were animals, and pulling out knives from their belts drew the blades across the children's throats. The priestess knelt below them. She held a silver dish beneath their necks and the children's blood flowed into it.

She then held the dish up above her head and addressed her audience.

'*Spirit take revenge.*'

Lucia felt an odd overwhelming feeling of strength and bravery, of fickle uncaringness. She rushed into the centre of the crowd and flung herself round like a whirling dervish, screaming as the crowd, the priestess, the sacrificed children

133

disappeared before her eyes, as she ran through them. She woke up in her bed in a cold sweat. It was dawn.

Simon and Grace were in the crypt, collecting up Grace's few belongings, when Lucia entered, breathless. It was still early morning.

'You must both hide in the secret room. We are all in danger.' Her eyes were wild.

Lucia led them quickly across the island to the oil room. She opened up the door to the secret room, frightened of what she might find inside. The room had returned to its previous form; Lucia removed the sheets and implements of childbirth from the room, pulling the eroded chain from the wall. Leaving provisions which would last them for a couple of days, she shut the door on them. There was such an intense purposiveness about her that they did not protest.

Death was everywhere Cameron looked. It was at the bottom of the steps. At the bottom of the sea. It was all around him, lying in wait. Death was in the midst of life. The previous day he had looked around at the others and wondered how they could move with such ease, how they could not see Death lurking there, licking his lips, how they could not negotiate around him but walk blindly straight through him.

Once Cameron had started to see death everywhere, he began to walk more awkwardly, more circuitously, walk into a room at an angle. He began to wonder if Lucia was death, or an omen of death. Nothing existed untainted, nothing did not have the resonance of the arbitrariness of life. Things lost their own properties.

Even the beauty of the sun over the sea reminded him of death, reminded him of transience. He watched the huge orange sun lower itself into the flat black sea and wished that it would not have to rise again so that he would not have to watch its death again.

He wrote in his diary as if the words would be an amulet against death.

It is difficult to stay alive when I have the memories I have inside of me. How can I live with what I have done when I don't know yet what I am capable of doing? This woman who has arrived on the island. Is she atonement or punishment? I don't know which. She looks hungry for something. Maso-maso: it will not fit. I can sense the malignant presence. Watching me, wanting to do me harm.

We are all possessed on this island. Lucia by her forgotten history, Grace by the death of her mother, Charlotte by her secret knowledge, Simon by his animism and me by my God.

He closed the diary. He was not capable of writing much. More often than not he was overwhelmed by the desire *not* to say something. For him, it was inarticulacy which was absolute.

135

Over the next few days, Cameron was frightened of falling into the sea of his melancholy again, where he felt as if he were drowning on dry land. Melancholy seemed beguiling and he had to struggle against giving up, giving over to drowning. Sometimes he felt that breathing was too much of an effort for him. The sea outside looked like the literal version of his state of mind, and at his worst moments he felt confused between the interior world and the exterior. As if everywhere he looked his interior world was reflected back at him.

Cameron tried to pull himself together, tried to turn his melancholy into simple ennui. He tried to grasp on to the appearance of the world.

He retired to his room. In his diary he wrote:

In voodoo the object and spirit become indistinguishable. A hair is a fragment of a person's spirit. Owning another's hair means having their spirit, the power over life and death.

He then placed a single strand of hair between the pages of his diary and shut the book.

Lucia quietly descended the steps to the oil room. She unlocked the door to the secret room. It had been five days since she had hidden them in there. Grace was lying sleeping on the bed. Simon was sitting on the wooden chair, as if keeping watch over her. Lucia handed him some food and water.

'What is happening on this island, Simon?' she asked.

'The evil spirit of the slave ship is acting as a force for good: it is enacting revenge, meting out a poetic justice. Just as Cameron's spirituality is leading to his damnation. Evil needs its opposite. Without light there is no darkness. Without darkness there is no light. Lucifer needs a God and without evil what would God mean? Evil and goodness are part of the same thing, no matter how hard you try to divide them. Madness lies in trying to separate them out.'

In his room, Cameron took out a small wooden box from his drawer. It contained a few dried plants. He dextrously extricated the seeds from the plants and with his clenched fist beat them into a powder. He opened up his diary. A single strand of red hair lay across the page as if the text had been cut by a fine wound. He added the hair to the seed compound.

He knew what to do to add to the compound's potency. He had learnt from Grace's mother the art of Obeah. He took a handful of the powder and flung it over his eyes. The powder stung his retinas but he refrained from washing it away. He had been taught that ritual was paramount in voodoo. After a few minutes the powder had melted into the membranes of his eyes.

Folding the rest of the powder into a piece of paper and slipping it into his pocket, he went down to the kitchen. Charlotte had just finished cooking their supper.

'You sit down now, Charlotte. I will serve the fish.'

Normally Charlotte served Cameron, and this inversion of power discomforted her. She felt it was not in Cameron's nature to serve.

Cameron sat down opposite her. Charlotte, Cameron thought, had never looked more beautiful. Her hair hung in curls about her face like a scarlet mist and her eyes reflected the flames of the candlelight. And she had that unfinished look. Charlotte began to eat. Cameron pulled the chain from his pocket with his watch attached to it and looked at its face.

Charlotte, having taken a few mouthfuls of the fish, put down her fork. She stood up suddenly, putting her hand to her throat, scattering the remains of the meal on to the ground.

'*What have you done?*' she whispered. Her body began to writhe in pain.

Cameron remained sitting, watching her, as if observing a macabre dance performed for his sole amusement. Charlotte opened her mouth to speak but no words came out. She collapsed on to the floor, her limbs trembling as if in an ecstatic trance. A few minutes later, her body fell still.

Cameron stood up and went over to her, and bending down hauled her body up and propped it back on the chair. He softly rearranged her hair around her face. She looked composed. Now he had silenced her, she looked completed.

Cameron's vision that night was becoming increasingly cloudy: the world seemed to be hiding behind a veil of mist. He wrote in his diary:

In voodoo there is no beginning and no end. Instead there is a dispersal of power, character and matter that constitute being – those three things can be interchanged.

Voodoo pulls slavery apart and reassembles it in a different order so white man becomes slave and black man the master.

So voodoo has put a curse upon me. I can feel evil all around me. My eyes are losing their sight. But I will not be susceptible. I will not submit to voodoo superstition, its powers of persuasion. For I am stronger than superstition. The strength of my belief will see me through. My lightness against their darkness.

Charlotte was always present at breakfast, either preparing, serving or eating with them. The next morning, when

Lucia came down to the kitchen, Charlotte was not there. There was just Cameron sitting there at breakfast. As if nothing was wrong.

'Where's Charlotte?'

Cameron didn't look up from his breakfast.

'There was an emergency. She had to leave the island.'

'Why?' She tried to sound nonchalant.

'She took ill suddenly. It was very calm. She left in the boat. I shan't expect her for a while.'

He was obviously lying. But whatever had happened to Charlotte, it now seemed Lucia was alone on the island with Cameron. Simon and Grace were still hidden down below in the oil room.

She looked out to sea. There was no trace of the burning ship.

'Something missing, Lucia?' Cameron asked coldly.

She swirled around. Too fast. 'No, no. Nothing missing.'

'It's up to us to keep the light burning. The light revolving, Lucia,' Cameron said. 'A lot of responsibility.' He seemed to be muttering in a way she had not seen before. He seemed defeated. 'I must return to my texts.'

For the first day he didn't leave his room. She asked him through the closed door if he wanted anything to eat but there was no reply. She looked through the crack in the door and saw him writing furiously. She heard him mutter, as he wrote, 'I am the Logos which dwells in the inexpressible light. I alone am inexpressible, undefiled, immeasurable, inconceivable Word.'

140

When he came down for supper, which she now dutifully prepared, his eyes seemed distant; he hardly seemed to notice her.

'When will Charlotte be coming back?' she asked.

'Who is Charlotte?'

She looked at him. She went into his dark blue eyes. He was not pretending.

As they ate, he said out of the blue of their silence:

'Stop saying that.'

'I said nothing.'

'I wasn't talking to you.'

'Who were you talking to?'

'The Devil, who is the architect of this world. He insists that I am on his side now. I have told him that he has made a terrible mistake and that I am on the side of the Angel of Light. I have told him all about my Faith. That has sustained me, unwaveringly, for the past ten years. He says that my Faith is just more words in my head. He insists that my soul is still captive to this earthly world and that I belong to his domain.'

He buried his head in his hands.

'I'll take over your watch,' she said.

She went upstairs to the light room and watched the lens turn, the light fall over the water.

Cameron rubbed his eyes harder, but this only caused them to hurt further. The whites of his eyes had become inflamed with blood. He decided to go upstairs to rest. Lying on his bed he closed his eyes and fell asleep.

His dream was feverish and intense. It was also real. For he was dreaming of what had happened on Jacob's Rock ten years ago. He was dreaming of history.

He dreamt that it was nearly dawn and he was keeping watch in the lantern room. His eyelids were beginning to droop. He did not ring the bell to waken his sleeping assistant, but instead tried to fight off the tiredness. He tried to resist the natural impulse of sleep. It seemed that he fell into oblivion for only a moment. But when he awoke it was to see the slave ship *Lucia* floundering on the reef, the captain and four of his crew, having abandoned ship, already rowing towards Jacob's Rock.

There was a terrible silence. The beat of the lighthouse's heart had stopped. The light had gone out while he slept. Cameron had stood up from his chair and opened his mouth to scream, but nothing had come out, and it was as if he were gasping in wonder.

Cameron woke from his dream, with a jerk, and opened his eyes. The room had fallen pitch black. The candle by his bedside had gone out. Suppressing his panic, for he did not like being in the dark, Cameron stretched out his hand for the candle. The palm of his hand felt flame. The candle was still alight.

Cameron leapt from his bed and staggered over to the window. For the second time, he saw no light light up the sea. But neither could he see moon nor stars. There was nothing. The world had turned black. But he could hear the click, click, clicking of the pendulum as the light turned round on its wheels, shining a silver path on to the sea.

Voodoo had made him blind. Cameron began to talk to himself relentlessly. His gnostic ideas became a repeated statement of belief. 'I am one of the elect. I am not doomed to darkness like the others, not destined to live in a world of ignorance and uncertainty. For error is empty and has nothing inside.'

His blindness made him even more reclusive. Lucia walked into his room once to bring him soup and saw him in the process of taking a spoonful of liquid, and she quickly withdrew before he realized she was there. He had begun taking laudanum.

Later, he told her he had started work on an interpretation of the Book of Revelations. He would ask her to sit by his bed and take notes.

Afterwards, she would feel exhausted and need to go into the light room and watch the light sway over the sea for comfort, hypnotized into a state of peace, waiting for the relief boat, not knowing when it would come, not knowing what had happened to Charlotte, and knowing Simon and Grace were locked up in the oil room. Only Cameron knew that the arrival of the relief boat was not weeks but months away.

This text of the Revelations was disturbing, verging on madness, Lucia thought, a madman's dream. And she felt susceptible to words on the island, as if its isolation and domination by the natural world gave added potency to man-made language. The Book of Revelations held a clue to her past, somewhere in the text, and as he dictated the book to her, she felt something of her own self was being uncovered which caused her heart to beat faster.

Something compelled her to continue taking down Cameron's words. As if she were on the right path to finding out who she really was.

'There is a light within a man of light, and it lights up the whole world. If it does not shine he is in darkness,' Cameron quoted. Then he would mutter, 'All these words, they form part of the chains to this material world. Words are part of the world's huge unreality. There is only Logos: the divine word. All other words are trinkets. Are you taking this down, Lucia? *Take it down!*'

The light in his mind was too much for him and Cameron would howl out. His face contorted upwards, as if lifted up by pain, and his eyes rolled in their sockets, and he started to speak an incantation, an odd language which seemed incomprehensible but which seemed to Lucia to have a logic and grammar of its own. He spoke this magic language as he used to speak the words of the Bible, with an intensity, just under his breath. And this incantation disturbed Lucia more than the physical contortions and possession he was undergoing. The physical transformation seemed arbitrary compared to this new language, which sounded the same as the Bible but whose meaning had darkness on its side.

With ease, his mouth and lips spoke the words, got round their odd sibilance, a little saliva frothing at the corner of his mouth, the lips rapidly moving up and down and from side to side as if his mouth had its own animistic momentum, driven by its own internal force, without any external motive.

When he did this, the rest of his body remained completely still like stone, simply his mouth moving in an inanimate body. It was as if all his energy and life force had been focused on his mouth, as if his moving mouth had drained the life from the rest of his body and the strength of the power of his mouth had dragged his body's vitality towards itself, like a whirlpool, a centrifugal force.

And she remembered that his sensual mouth, even when it was speaking its holy text, always seemed to have a force that subverted its spiritual utterances.

And now its sensuality had transformed into an insane incoherence, a passion which the mouth could not subvert. His sensuality had turned against itself, transformed into violence, become its own worst enemy. And she realized this was what true darkness was. She only had to look at his face to see the darkness clouding it, in spite of his pallid skin; there even seemed to be darkness in the room, but the sun was shining through the window and seagulls floated outside in the blue sky.

Days passed and still there was no sign of the relief boat. Lucia continued to smuggle food and drink down to where Simon and Grace were hiding in the secret room. Lucia was growing more and more worried. Walking along the shore, to gain a respite, the strong, sweet scent of death caught her nostrils and drew her in the direction of the crypt.

Lucia descended the stone steps of the crypt, slowly. She stood in the entrance and looked into the cavernous space. Lying on the centre of the empty stone floor was the body of Charlotte. A note had been pinned to the front of Charlotte's dress, written in Cameron's slanted angular handwriting.

Non venit mutare conditiones sed mentes.

Lucia ran across the island into the lighthouse and up to Cameron's room. She knocked on his door. There was no answer and she tried the handle. It was unlocked. She opened the door and entered. The whole room was filled with paper covered in reams of his tiny angular hand-writing.

There were also pages of the notes she had taken for him from the Book of Revelations in her own handwriting. Bibles were spread out over the floor, pages ripped out and attached to the wall. She read some of his words. It was meaningless. Just words strung together, blasphemous words, banal words, biblical phrases, bits of conversation they had shared at dinner. It was a giant depiction of his life with the meaning taken out: no narrative, no analysis, no thought. Just excerpts.

The District Superintendent lingered over that space between sea and land, water then rock. And then in the distance a light. And then gone. A space of certain seconds and then the twinkle of light again. At first it seemed as if it was part of his imagination. Something out of the corner of his eye that actually didn't exist at all. A few seconds of wondering. Then confirmation again. A light in the distance in the sea. So far away that nothing else was visible. A light like the explosion of a star. A flicker and out. Only the rigour and exactness of the time between implied that it was man-made, that it was not an act of nature. Through the soft haze of a winter's day. Through the blue sky and the white opaque mist.

The Superintendent and his crew arrived to find the blind Cameron, unclothed, sitting on the floor of the lantern room, muttering, as if he were watching the lens revolve. They found the decaying body of Charlotte in the mausoleum and the confession lying out in Charlotte's room. They could not find the woman who had written the message in the bottle that had brought them here, weeks before the relief boat was due.

They heard shouts from the oil room and going down, discovered the secret door. They opened it and Simon and Grace emerged, shaken but unharmed, their supplies having run out only a few days ago. The Superintendent saw the silhouette of a female figure appear at the balcony and then disappear into the air.

The Superintendent rowed Simon and Grace over to the sailing boat the next day. As they looked back towards the lighthouse, Simon said to the girl:

'You know, Grace, that Lucia was the evil spirit of the slave ship that went down ten years ago. Your mother used your mouth to summon her up. You have been your mother's host. The very spirit you were trying to destroy was being summoned up by you without you realizing.'

Grace looked upset.

'So my mother used me?'

'No. It was her way of bridging the gap between life and death. Of continuing life through you. She used me too. It was my hands which touched the figurehead of the ship. I brought Lucia to life.'

'How do you know all this, Simon? You seem to understand everything that has happened.'

'Magic understands magic.'

Cameron Black was arrested for aiding and abetting illegal slave trading. He ended his days in a lunatic asylum. Simon returned to the west coast of Scotland where he took up farming again. He formally adopted Grace as his daughter. Having abandoned the island, his magical powers left him.

One afternoon, soon after having returned from school, Grace found a corner of woodland out of sight of the farm and sat down cross-legged in front of the small wooden fetish she had brought with her from the island.

In her own voice she addressed it:

'So, Mother, are you finished with me, your own flesh and blood? Is it all finished at last?'

And in her mother's deep voice she answered her own question:

'Voodoos never finish anything. If we say we have finished, it is not true. Everything remains unfinished.'

The Northern Lighthouse Board appointed three new keepers for Jacob's Rock. They arrived at the lighthouse one by one over the following months. They grew used to seeing the ghost of a woman with wild grey eyes and long black hair walking down the steps of the lighthouse, standing on the peninsula as the tide was coming in or looking out over the sea from the edge of the cliff. They could hear her murmuring in the dark, exhorting them to save her. But sometimes they would hear her singing, content with her lot.

The ghostly spirit still did not know who she was or where she had come from. But she roamed the lighthouse now waiting for someone to claim her, to tell her who she was and why she was there.

ACKNOWLEDGEMENTS

During the writing of *Pharos*, the words of slaves recorded by Julius Lester in *To Be A Slave* (Scholastic Inc., New York, 1968) were occasionally used.

The writing of *Pharos* was facilitated by a Creative Scotland Award (supported by the Scottish Arts Council National Lottery Fund).

Thank you to my editor and publisher Lennie Goodings, and to my agent Jonny Geller.